"It was a long time ago. Let's put it all behind us."

"There's a snag," said James in a tone that quickened her pulse. "Now I've seen you again it doesn't feel like a long time ago."

"Nevertheless," Rose said woodenly, "it is." It was impossible to behave or sound natural when the mere touch of James Sinclair's hand on hers was rousing feelings she had never experienced in the most passionate of lovemaking with anyone else. And James knew it, she realized, as she met the blaze of triumph in his eyes.

"Rose." He smiled slowly, and brushed a lock of hair back from her face. "Surely a kiss goodbye is permissible in the circumstances?" He drew her resisting body into his arms and kissed her, taking his time over it, the shape and taste and touch of his lips so frighteningly familiar she had no defense against the hot, consuming pleasure of the kiss.

CATHERINE GEORGE was born in Wales, and early on developed a passion for reading, which eventually fueled her compulsion to write. Marriage to an engineer led to nine years of living in Brazil, but on her husband's later travels the education of her son and daughter kept her in the U.K. And instead of constant reading to pass her lonely evenings she began to write the first of her romantic novels. When not writing and reading she loves to cook, listen to opera and browse in antique shops.

Books by Catherine George

Catherine George

HUSBAND FOR REAL

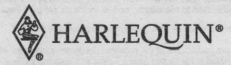

TORONTO • NEW YORK • LONDON
AMSTERDAM • PARIS • SYDNEY • HAMBURG
STOCKHOLM • ATHENS • TOKYO • MILAN • MADRID
PRAGUE • WARSAW • BUDAPEST • AUCKLAND

ISBN 0-373-12225-X

HUSBAND FOR REAL

First North American Publication 2002.

Visit us at www.eHarlequin.com

Printed in U.S.A.

CHAPTER ONE

WHEN a crimson envelope arrived among the morning post she was amused at first. But her smile faded when she took out an unsigned Valentine card painted with a single red rose. Frowning, she examined the typed envelope, but the postmark was so illegible it gave no clue to the sender's identity.

Rose stood lost in thought for a moment or two, then took her usual stack of mail into the small office at the back of the bookshop and propped the card up conspicuously as something to joke about. Which it had to be. She dismissed it with a shrug, switched on lights, computer and point of sale, chose some Schubert for background music and unlocked the door, ready for the first customers of the day.

As usual these were mostly mothers straight from the school run, needing books for their young. For the first half-hour Rose was kept busy looking out the required titles, or ordering them for delivery next day, at the same time exchanging conversation and offering opinions on the newest craze in children's stories or the latest paperback fiction. Interest in her customers, coupled with pleasant personal service, which came easy to Rose, were a necessary asset for a privately owned bookshop, even if in Chastlecombe only the supermarket and the various newsagents offered anything by way of competition.

When Rose's friend arrived for her part-time stint at the shop she crowed with laughter when she spotted the card.

'Lucky old you! I'm envious, boss. My beloved isn't

the sentimental kind.' Bel Cummings's eyes sparkled as she made the fresh pot of coffee they tried to share before she started. 'I suppose it's from Anthony. Though I would have expected something more impressive—'

'In the unimaginable event of his sending me one at all at his age,' Rose finished for her.

Bel smiled in full agreement. 'So who's the secret lover, then?'

'Haven't a clue.'

'Then it must be Anthony,' said her friend, disappointed. 'Get the thumbscrews out and make him confess over dinner. You are seeing him this weekend?'

'Yes, but tonight for a change. He's tied up with Marcus tomorrow.' Rose finished her coffee quickly. 'Right. I'd better get on with this lot before the day's book consignment arrives.'

After Bel went off to greet a customer Rose began to sort out bills and invoices from the usual heap of junk-mail, feeling out of sorts as she worked. And, though the anonymous card was mostly to blame, some of her mood was reluctance to break her routine. She preferred Friday nights on her own. After an hour or so's paperwork she liked to linger in the bath, eat something easy on a tray in front of her television and get to bed early with one of the latest additions to stock. But this weekend Anthony's teenage son would be home alone. Marcus had stayed in Chastlecombe with his mother after the divorce. And because Liz Garrett was spending this weekend away, her ex-husband, determined to keep his son happy at all costs, would devote Saturday as well as his usual Sunday to him.

Rose liked Marcus well enough, and from the little she knew of him didn't think he actively resented her. It surprised her that a young teenager preferred his father's company to going out with friends, but she was perfectly happy for Anthony to spend Saturday night with his son. Tonight, too, if she were honest. Her week had been gratifyingly busy, and by the time she finished work she wouldn't feel like dressing up and dining out. Her original offer of supper for two upstairs in her flat—a first in their relationship—had been turned down in favour of a table at Chastlecombe's most fashionable restaurant.

Rose had known Anthony Garrett by sight when she was in her teens, but she met him again socially just after his divorce came through. He was an accountant promoted from a small Chastlecombe branch to the London head office of his company. And since the divorce he came back to stay at the King's Head on some weekends, to see his son and spend all the Saturday evenings with Rose that she would allow. She was well aware that Anthony's choice of someone local to wine and dine was deliberate. The injured party in his failed marriage, he'd remained firmly entrenched in a circle of friends only too ready to inform the ex-Mrs Garrett of every known detail of his connection with the new young manager of Dryden Books. Anthony was openly proud of his relationship with an attractive woman so much younger than himself. And if Rose sometimes felt like a trophy, it amused more than annoyed her.

Lunch-hour was busy, as usual, and it was late before Bel could be persuaded to go out for something to eat. During the post-lunch lull Rose finished checking the consignment of books newly arrived that morning, sorted out customer orders to file on the shelves kept for the purpose, then went into the office to eat the sandwich Bel brought for her when she got back.

It was Rose's habit to catch up on reading from new stock over lunch, and she was chuckling over one of the latest children's books when Bel popped her head round the door.

'Delivery for you, boss.'

'I'm not expecting anything—' Rose stared in surprise when Bel handed over a long, beribboned package. Then swallowed convulsively when she took out a long-stemmed crimson rose.

'Hey, are you all right?' said Bel in alarm.

'Ate my lunch too quickly.'

'I think the rose was meant to be romantic, not give you indigestion,' teased Bel. 'Who's it from?'

'Let's find out.' Rose picked up the phone to ask the local florist.

'No idea, sorry,' was the response. 'Your secret admirer pushed a typed note through the door this morning, with instructions and the exact amount of money.'

When Rose rang off Bel patted her shoulder in concern. 'Are you all right, boss? You've been a bit abstracted all day.'

'I'm fine.' Rose eyed the flower with dislike. 'But I detest mysteries. If all this Valentine nonsense is Anthony's idea I'll have words with him tonight.'

'But surely he would have phoned the order through in the usual way?'

'He's got plenty of contacts in the town. Anyone could have put the money through the door of the flower shop for him.'

'Well I think it's *very* romantic,' declared Bel, then left to deal with an influx of customers, and Rose shut the door on her mystery tribute and went off to help.

After Rose locked up for the night she scanned through the pile of invoices and school orders waiting to be dealt in the office, hesitated, then abandoned her Friday routine.

She would be alone for Saturday evening this week. The paperwork could wait until then.

The phone rang when she arrived upstairs, but when she picked up the receiver the only sound on the line was heavy breathing.

'Who *is* this?' she demanded angrily. A voice whispered her name, raising the hairs on her neck, then the line went dead. Shaken and furious, Rose punched in the numbers to identify her caller, but the number had been withheld. Some stupid fool playing a prank, she assured herself, and made herself some lethally strong coffee to calm herself down.

She filled an empty milk bottle with water, thrust the rose in it and put it on the window-sill of her small kitchen, her eyes brooding as she gazed at the beautiful, perfect bloom. A rose for Rose, said a voice in her mind. A male voice. With the merest hint of Scots. Odd. She could hear the voice so plainly its owner could have been in the room with her. But normally she flatly refused to allow herself the indulgence of thinking about him. The wretched Valentine card was to blame, reminding her of things best forgotten. The phone-call hadn't helped, either. But the rose was the real culprit. Its relentless, heady scent brought memories rushing back like persistent ghosts determined to haunt her. And, as she got ready for the evening, for the first time in years Rose let them stay.

Rose Dryden had gone off to university just after her eighteenth birthday. Eager to embrace everything student life had to offer, she'd been a little wary at first when she'd found she was to share a college flat with two girls who'd been to school together. Cornelia Longford and Fabia Dennison, both a year older than Rose, possessed an aura of self-confidence she envied. But they were warm, friendly creatures who had taken their younger flat-mate under their combined wing, and from the first had seen to it that Rose took full advantage of every social diversion college life had to offer.

Rose, grateful to be accepted as part of a trio, had quickly become accustomed to evenings spent in the students' union with a boisterous, rowdy crowd of both sexes. Envious at first of Con's blonde, thoroughbred looks, or the brain Fabia kept hidden behind a flippant manner, even their names, which were so much more glamorous than her own, Rose had quickly blossomed in their company. By the end of term she'd attended every possible festivity available, including the Christmas ball, and had been as ready as any of her peers to contribute to heated discussions on how to improve the world.

Determined to get a good degree, Rose had worked hard. But at the same time she'd learned how to make half a pint of lager last all evening, how to flirt, and how to avoid danger when some importunate male misread the signals.

'It's common-sense,' Con assured her. 'If you fancy a bloke you go out on a twosome. If you don't, stick with the crowd.'

Rose never let on that the only men in her life up to that point had been friends of her unmarried aunt, plus one or two brothers of girls from school. Nevertheless, she had enough common-sense to know that a twosome might involve a lot more than just a pizza and a trip to the cinema. And, because she wasn't attracted to anyone enough to risk finding out, her attitude challenged those among the male student body who considered themselves irresistible.

'Idiots,' said Rose irritably, during the first days back after Christmas. 'I just don't fancy any of them that way.'

'You will, eventually,' warned Fabia, immersed in painting her toenails different colours. 'Mother Nature gets us all in the end. You'll see. One look across a crowded room and, wham, you're done for.'

Rose giggled. 'No way—not me!'

'She's right, you know.' Con looked up from her books. 'But most of them just want a fun night out, plus some hanky-panky at the end of it if they're lucky.' She paused dramatically. 'The trick is to make one of them fall in love so violently he'll be your slave.'

Fabia collapsed with laughter, lying flat on her bed with her legs in the air as she waggled her toes to dry them.

'You can't *make* someone fall in love with you, Con,' said Rose scornfully.

'How do you know? Have you ever tried?'

'Well, no, but—'

'Then keep quiet and listen.' Con's smile sent shivers down Rose's spine. 'Come sit at Mama's knee, children, and imbibe the knowledge. I'm the neurobiologist, remember, and this is scientific stuff. I read about it while I was having my hair cut yesterday. It's a proper game plan. No black magic involved,' she added, laughing. 'You don't need eye of newt or anything, Rosie, so don't look at me like that! Trust me. Are you two game?'

Fabia nodded so eagerly that Rose, afraid that dissent would be taken as cowardice, gave a reluctant nod.

'Good girl, Rosie,' approved Con. 'Don't look so worried. This will be fun.'

The first step was for each of the trio to write four men's names on separate pieces of paper, and put the folded scraps into a hat.

'Now we shake it up and draw one out—only one each, mind, and if we hit on the same one as someone else we draw again,' instructed Con.

The three of them thrust fingers into the hat simultaneously but Con raised a peremptory hand before they opened them.

'This needs a bit of ceremony. You first, Fabia.'

'Will Hargreaves,' announced Fabia with satisfaction, then grinned at the other two. 'I didn't cheat, honest. Just luck of the draw.'

Con groaned as she read hers. 'Joe Kidd.'

'But he's been chasing you ever since freshers' week,' objected Rose. 'That's no contest—' She stopped dead, her face flushing crimson as she saw the name on her own slip.

'Who on earth have you got?' demanded Con, taking the paper from her. 'Crikey—James Sinclair.' She raised an eyebrow at Fabia, who shrugged defensively.

'Why not? You said any name we like.'

'So we did,' agreed Rose, the light of battle in her eyes. 'Luck of the draw, just as you said. The legendary Sinclair is only captain of the rugby team and so brilliant he's bound to get a double first—not to mention being a good looking hunk *and* in his finals' year. Piece of cake. I'll have him slavering after little old first-year me in no time.' She thrust her hands through her hair in despair.

Con patted her shoulder soothingly. 'Steady on. You don't have to go through with it if you don't want to.'

'Of course not—it was just my stupid joke,' said Fabia, remorseful now. 'Pick another name, Rosie; you can't possibly go after Sinclair.'

'Why not?' demanded Rose hotly. 'You don't think I'm sexy enough to attract a man like him, I suppose!'

'*No*, love! It's not that.' Fabia hesitated. 'The thing is, rumour has it he might be gay.'

'That's just gossip, because he doesn't chase after every female in sight,' scolded Con.

Rose sighed glumly. 'Any female at all, the way I hear it.'

'How do you know?'

'When I went to a rugby match with Ally Farmer—she's going out with the full-back—she told me that Sinclair isn't interested in women.'

The other two exchanged a look.

'I'd forgotten you liked rugby,' said Con thoughtfully.

'I went to a couple of matches when you two were off shopping...' Rose trailed into silence, eyes suspicious as the others looked at her in speculation. 'What?'

'Sinclair must have seen you,' Fabia pointed out.

'Transfixed by my beautiful blue eyes while he was charging up the field with half the opposing team hanging from every limb,' said Rose scathingly. 'I wish!'

Con, diverted, tilted Rose's chin up. 'He could have been, they're big enough, *and* unusual, sort of navy blue.'

'Nice,' agreed Fabia. 'But, as I keep saying, you should use some paint on them, Rosie, you don't do them justice.'

'They've got twenty-twenty vision, just the same, and I assure you that the mighty Sinclair did *not* notice me.'

'He will if we carry out the plan scientifically,' Con assured her, 'so here's what we do...'

Rose crawled into bed that night utterly convinced of her own insanity. Because she had flatly refused to renege on the task of ensnaring James Sinclair, Con and Fabia had abandoned their part in the scheme in favour of forming a back-up team for the project Rose had referred to as mission impossible. According to Con it would have been child's play to enslave Messrs Hargreaves and Kidd. Sinclair, on the other hand, constituted a challenge Rose could hardly be expected to tackle single-handed. So Con and Fabia would research every last thing about Sinclair's tastes, family background and relevant details, taking care not to give the game away. Then when Rose was in Sinclair's actual company—a prospect that rendered Rose sick with apprehension at the mere thought of it—she could drop casual phrases into the conversation that would indicate like tastes and interests of her own, and thus convince him she was a soul-mate.

But first, Con had instructed, Rose must run into Sinclair by accident.

'Where?' demanded Rose.

'When I said "run" I meant it,' said Con ruthlessly. 'At the stadium the town council lets us use. Get yourself there early in the morning. Very early. Joe Kidd says Sinclair runs at the track there most mornings about seven before anyone else does.'

'I have to *run*?' gasped Rose.

'At seven?' said Fabia, equally horrified.

'Rose must be there well before that,' said Con cruelly. 'He must come upon *her* by chance, not the other way round.'

'Not *much* before,' wailed Rose. 'Or I'll be dead before he even gets there.'

Tossing and turning in her bed, Rose decided that the whole scheme was madness. In the morning she'd tell the others she'd changed her mind. She fell asleep at last for what felt like a split second before Con was shaking her awake again, deaf to all protests as she thrust her victim into a track-suit, found socks and trainers and, while Rose pulled them on, twisted the tumbled black hair into a hasty plait. Con crammed a scarlet sweat-band low over Rose's eyes, then pushed her out of the door.

'Coffee when you come back,' she promised in a whisper.

'*If* I come back,' said Rose bitterly.

The stadium was deserted when she got there. She brightened. Perhaps he'd gone already. It was a grey, damp day, but thankfully no actual rain. Praying that Sinclair wouldn't turn up for once, Rose jogged up and down on the spot for a bit, then with zero enthusiasm began to run round the track. Three times max, she promised herself, then back to bed, no matter what. For the first circuit Rose, unaccustomed to serious running, thought she might possibly expire before she completed it. But during the second lap she gradually mastered the art of breathing and running at the same time and felt a little better. Then she heard footsteps behind her, and her heart lodged in her throat and she could hardly breathe at all. She stared straight ahead, the breath whistling through her lungs as a tall figure in a dark track suit ran past, eyes turned towards her for an instant. Sinclair acknowledged her existence with the slightest of nods, then raced on down the track.

Now her quarry was in sight, flowing round the track with coordinated grace, Rose summoned up her last shreds of stamina to keep going. Instead of leaving at the next exit she ran on to make another circuit of the track to allow the legendary Sinclair to lap her. This time he gave her a fleeting smile as he passed, and Rose, feeling she'd done all, and more, that could be expected of her, left Sinclair to it and dragged herself back to the flat, hoping her heart would slow down to a normal beat some time in the foreseeable future.

'Mission...accomplished.' She panted, chest heaving.

Con and Fabia pounced on her with cries of delight, demanded every detail, then hustled her off to shower.

'Can't have you too stiff to run next time,' said Con firmly.

'Next time?' gasped Rose. 'I've got to do this again?'

'Yes. But not tomorrow. Give him a day to miss you.'

'Oh come *on*! He barely noticed me.'

'Trust us older women, Rosie,' said Fabia, grinning. 'Sinclair will look for you tomorrow.'

The night before her next run Rose stayed in. 'If I'm running in the morning I need an early night,' she told the others. 'And I've got a tutorial tomorrow, so I must finish this essay, anyway. Try not to wake me when you come in tonight.'

Con woke her at six-thirty the following morning instead. 'Come *on*, Rose,' she whispered, shaking her. 'Up you get.'

Once again Rose was bundled, yawning, into running gear, but this time she'd braided her hair the night before, and only had to brush her teeth and throw cold water on her face before Con thrust her out into the chilly morning like a mother sending a reluctant child off to school.

Rose arrived at the stadium a little earlier than before, but this time Sinclair was there before her. She cursed him in fulminating silence. Now she'd have to run extra laps just to save face. The familiar, lean figure soon flowed past with its usual grace, and a slight smile came her way before Sinclair raced off into the distance, gathering speed. Rose gritted her teeth and pounded doggedly on until sweat soaked from her hair into the towelling band and each breath was like a spear through the ribs. Her running companion lapped her with increasing ease, but Rose forced herself to look straight ahead, counting the circuits until the magic number four released her from torture and she could escape.

This time the others were worried when Rose collapsed, crimson-faced and sweating, on Con's bed.

'No need to kill yourself, love,' said Fabia, pulling her shoes off.

'Was he there?' demanded Con.

'Of—course he—was there!' Rose heaved in a deep breath, eyeing the others malevolently. 'Before me. I had to do *four* circuits.'

'Brilliant,' crowed Fabia. 'Think how fit you'll be— and I bet he noticed you this time.'

'He could hardly fail to; he lapped me often enough.' Rose dragged herself up, groaning. 'Right. For pity's sake make me some coffee while I shower, please.'

Rose was allowed a run-free morning next day, purely, Con decreed, because it was a Saturday, and she could watch Sinclair play rugby in the afternoon instead. 'And just to fog the issue a bit we'll come with you, and cheer on Will Hargreaves. Someone's injured, so Will's got a place on the team today. *So* useful.'

Fabia was all for Rose turning up in her running clothes, complete with red sweat-band, so Sinclair would remember her, but Con wouldn't hear of it.

'Much too obvious. Rose can wear whatever she usually wears to stand ankle-deep in mud in a howling wind. Oh, how I wish it was summer, and Sinclair played cricket!' She sighed regretfully. 'Actually the whole scheme would be better in hot weather. You could strip off a bit, Rose. When the male of the species registers bare female flesh he gives off more pheromones—'

'Stop it,' howled Rose. 'I don't want to know!'

Normally she bemoaned her lack of inches, but at the match she was only too pleased to tuck herself between her tall friends, with lanky Joe Kidd and a few more yelling males for cover as they cheered the home team on to victory over a neighbouring college. Sinclair, at outside half, played with a brilliance which roused a frenzy of

appreciation in his fans on the touchline, but Rose's
gloom deepened with every penalty he kicked between
the posts. If only she'd set out to capture some ordinary
mortal's interest she might have at least had *some* chance
of success. But with Sinclair she hadn't a hope. She could
just give up, of course. But her Dryden backbone stiffened
at the mere idea. When the referee blew the whistle after
Sinclair threw himself over the line to score a final try,
Rose watched the mud-covered hero leave the field sur-
rounded by shoulder-slapping team mates, and made herself a solemn vow. She would succeed. Somehow.

While the trio were thawing out over mugs of coffee
back in the flat later, Will Hargreaves rang with the news
that the rugby crowd would be in the Sceptre in the town
that night.

'Thanks, Will,' said Con triumphantly. 'Keep us a seat.'

Fabia turned to Rose with a militant gleam in her eye.
'Right. Let's get to work. By the time we finish with you,
Rosebud, the great Sinclair can't fail to notice you.'

Deaf to her protests, Con and Fabia curled up Rose's
newly-washed hair, bullied her into a skinny-ribbed
sweater of Con's and a pair of Rose's own denims dis-
carded as too tight. Then they sat her down in front of a
mirror and went to work on her face with the intentness
of Renaissance painters creating a masterpiece.

'My word,' exclaimed Fabia when they'd brushed
Rose's hair into a rippling waterfall down her back.
'Didn't we do well?'

Rose eyed her reflection with a touch of awe. Outlined
in black, violet shadow in the hollows, her eyes looked
larger in her small, triangular face, balancing the wide,
full-lipped mouth Con had outlined with a pencil then
painted with natural lip-gloss to leave the eyes to domi-
nate. 'I look so different—'

'You look gorgeous, Rose,' said Con, so obviously sincere that Rose relaxed.

'Not too much over the top?'

'No,' said Fabia, patting her shoulder. 'We just added a few touches. The basic material was there to start with.'

The Sceptre was crowded by the time they arrived, but Will and Joe had kept places for them at a corner table near the bar. Rose spotted her quarry the moment she arrived. The thick dark hair and honed bone structure of his face were unmistakable. Even laughing among a group of his friends he stood out from the rest; something so mature and self-contained about him Rose felt a sudden stab of panic, glad to slide into a seat with her back to the room.

'Don't look at him,' whispered Con. 'We'll tell you what to do next.'

'Dance on the table?' snapped Rose.

'If you like! But first I'll tell you when it's your round so you can go up to the bar.'

Rose suddenly regretted the cheeseburger she'd wolfed on the way back from the match. She smiled her thanks when Miles, one of her most faithful admirers, put a glass of lager in front of her, but the very thought of it made her gag. She turned to Joe Kidd determinedly and began to discuss the match, but for once Joe, normally a devotee of Con's, was more interested in chatting Rose up than talking rugby.

There was an unmistakable gleam in his eye as he looked her up and down. 'What have you done to yourself, Rosie? You look—'

'Back off, Joe,' whispered Con urgently, glaring at him. Then, in an undertone reminded Rose of her priorities. 'Sinclair's just gone up to the bar to get a round in. On your bike.'

'But we've all got drinks,' muttered Rose wildly.

'Buy some peanuts, or something.' Con tugged her to her feet. 'Go.'

Rose pushed her way through the crowd and, conscious that her eagle-eyed mentors were watching, managed to wriggle eventually into a space alongside Sinclair. He glanced down at her and, as instructed, Rose gave him a cool little smile, then looked away, stomach churning. Her heart leapt as she felt fingers brush her arm. Pulse racing, she turned to look up into eyes the colour of burnished pewter.

'Hello,' said Sinclair. 'Don't I know you?'

CHAPTER TWO

THE deep voice held a trace of Scots accent which did alarming things to Rose's knees. Heart thumping under the clinging pink sweater, she somehow managed to follow Con's instructions and frowned, pretending to think, but before she could mention the stadium he snapped his fingers.

'Pocahontas with the rope of hair!' he exclaimed, and gave her a slow smile which put a final end to any nonsense about giving up her scheme. 'I've seen you at the track.'

'Oh, right.' Rose returned the smile, deeply grateful that he hadn't needed a reminder. 'I'm not there often enough, I'm afraid.' She took the bull by the horns. 'I watched the match this afternoon, by the way. Congratulations.'

'Good game,' he agreed. 'You like rugby?'

Rose nodded, then drew his attention to the barman, who was waiting for payment. Before Sinclair handed over the money he turned to her in enquiry.

'Let me buy you a drink.'

'I already have one, thanks. I just wanted some nuts.' She gave a surreptitious glance at the table in the corner, where everyone was watching, riveted, as Sinclair insisted on paying for the packet of nuts Rose didn't want, signalled to a friend to take the tray of drinks away, then leaned against the bar with the air of a man prepared to linger.

'What's your name?' he asked.

Nerves rendered her answer so quiet Sinclair had to bend his head to hers.

'I didn't hear you.'

'Rose,' she said in his ear. 'Rose Dryden.'

'Mine's Sinclair.'

Fascinated to find he pronounced it to rhyme with 'sprinkler', Rose gave him a polite little smile, thanked him for the nuts, then went back to her table.

'That went off well,' said Con in her ear.

'Yes. He remembered me from the track.'

'I *knew* he would!'

Normally Rose would have enjoyed the evening, but suddenly the crowd she was with seemed immature and noisy, and the usual overtures from the male contingent, more persistent tonight due to her new look, failed to amuse. After an hour or so she'd had enough.

'I'm going,' she whispered to Con. 'Headache.'

'Want me to come with you?'

'No, it's early. You stay. I just need fresh air.' Rose chose a moment when everyone was embroiled in a heated argument, made for the cloakroom, then changed direction and slid through the exit door unnoticed.

Rose had never walked back to campus alone at night. As she left the town to climb the hill to the college she heard footsteps behind her and felt suddenly afraid. And at last began to run, her worst fears confirmed when someone began to run after her.

'Rose—Rose Dryden,' called an unmistakable voice, and she whirled round to find Sinclair gaining on her.

'Sorry,' she said breathlessly, and tried to smile, but her lips felt stiff. 'I didn't know it was you.'

'I saw you leave and came after you.' He wagged an admonishing finger. 'You shouldn't wander around alone at this time of night.'

'It's quite safe,' she said defensively.

'Then why did you run when I followed you?'

Rose shrugged. 'Instinct, I suppose.'

'I'll see you to your door. Are you in hall?'

'No, one of the college flats.' She fell into step with him, hardly able to believe her luck. Con and Fabia would be over the moon.

'So tell me about yourself,' ordered her companion. 'How old are you?'

For a moment Rose thought of lying, but something about James Sinclair decided her against it. 'Eighteen,' she admitted reluctantly, certain that from the lofty heights of twenty-two he would instantly lose interest. Then she remembered her coaching. 'And, if you want my CV, I'm reading English Literature, like foreign films, and go for the occasional run to keep fit. Sorry you asked?' she finished, laughing.

'Not at all.' He smiled down at her when they paused at the entrance to her building.

'How about you?' she said casually.

Sinclair hesitated, then gave her the information she already knew, that he was doing business studies and economics.

Time to go before he got bored. Rose smiled at him and held out her hand. 'Thank you for troubling to come after me. I appreciate it. Goodnight.'

His eyes narrowed in warning. 'Before you go, Rose Dryden, promise you won't walk home alone at night again.'

She nodded obediently.

'Say it,' he ordered.

'All right—I promise.'

'Good. See you on the track some time.' He shook the hand solemnly, gave her the slow-burning smile, and

Rose, heart thumping at the sight of it, managed a friendly little nod and went inside.

When Con arrived, earlier than usual, she checked to see Rose was awake, then beckoned Fabia into the room with her. 'Are you all right, Rose?'

'Fine.' She abandoned her book and sat up cross-legged on the bed, grinning like a Cheshire cat.

'Someone looks pleased with herself!' said Fabia, lolling at the foot of the bed. 'Mind you, I would be too, if Sinclair had bought *me* some nuts. Have you eaten them?'

Not for the world would Rose have admitted that the unopened packet was zipped safely away in her tote bag. 'I think I left them in the pub.'

Con settled herself in the room's only chair. 'Admit it, Rose, the plan's working like a charm.'

'Better than you think!' said Rose in jubilation.

The other girls stared, wide-eyed when they heard Sinclair had gone after her to see her home.

'Did he kiss you goodnight?' demanded Fabia.

'Of course not!' Rose smiled demurely. 'We shook hands.'

The other two laughed their heads off, then Con got up to make some coffee, respect in her eyes. 'I never thought you'd pull it off, you know. Sinclair's immunity to our sex is legendary.'

Rose pulled a face. 'I don't think he sees me as one of the opposite sex, exactly.'

Fabia shrieked with laughter. 'Are you kidding? With all that hair and the magnificent paint job we did, not to mention a shape to die for in that sexy little sweater of Con's—of *course* he thinks of you as a girl.'

'But a very young one,' said Rose, depressed. 'He gave me a right old lecture about walking home alone.'

Con was undeterred. 'Sinclair noticed you, remembered

you, wanted to buy you a drink, then came after you to make sure you were safe. Don't worry about the little girl aspect, ducky—remember Lolita!'

Embarking on phase two of Con's plan, Rose missed the next day's run, but after completing a third circuit in solitude the following morning had begun to think all the heart-pounding effort was in vain by the time the familiar athletic figure appeared. She returned the smile Sinclair gave her as he passed, completed the circuit, then left before he could lap her, or she fell in a heap. Whichever came first.

She wouldn't have admitted it to the others, but it was an effort of will to stay away from the track next morning. But none at all to stay in the same night.

'I must do some work,' she said firmly. Because Sinclair never patronised it, an evening at the students' union no longer held the same allure.

Rose no longer needed a morning call for her run. Next morning she was out of the room by six-thirty, shivering in the cold half-light as she hurried to the stadium, openly looking forward, now, to her early-morning glimpse of Sinclair. To her horror he was there before her again. She groaned. Now she'd have to do even more circuits just to keep up the myth that she liked running. She jogged up and down on the spot for a moment, to warn muscles of the coming ordeal, then started down the track at a speed moderate enough to give her any hope of staying the course long enough to look convincing.

When Sinclair passed her this time she was rewarded with a 'Hi!' to go with the smile as he went flying by.

'Hi,' panted Rose, and ran on, making no attempt to catch up with him. This, she soon found, wasn't necessary. The next time Sinclair caught up with her he slowed down and ran with her.

'Come on, try to speed up a little,' he exhorted, not even out of breath.

Rose did her best to obey, but after three gruelling circuits she flung up her hands in surrender and slumped down at the side of the track, her head on her knees as she tried to get her breath back.

Sinclair hunkered down beside her, looking concerned. 'Hey, sorry, Rose. I didn't mean to finish you off.'

She turned a crimson, sweating face up to his. 'I'm not—in your—class,' she gasped.

'You easily could be. Come every morning for a while. You'll soon get into shape. Not,' he added, with the smile that was no help to Rose in trying to breathe normally, 'that there's anything wrong with yours.'

She scrambled hastily to her feet, glad that her crimson face could hardly turn redder. 'Time I got back to shower.'

'Ah. You don't care for personal remarks.'

She liked his a lot. Rose smiled non-committally as he fell in step beside her, wondering if he meant to see her back to the flat again.

'I bring some kit and have a shower here sometimes when I've got lectures,' he said casually. 'If you do the same tomorrow we could have breakfast afterwards in the transport café down the hill.'

Rose felt a rush of excitement, wondering if this would be Con's idea of progress. Not that it mattered. By this time, plan or no plan, Rose Dryden was totally committed to her crusade to make the lofty, uninterested-in-women James Sinclair fall in love with her. Nothing was going to persuade her from it until she either succeeded, or he told her to get lost.

'If it doesn't appeal to you, don't worry,' he said curtly, and turned away.

Rose came to with a start. 'It appeals very much. I'd like that.'

'Right, then,' he said briskly. 'See you in the morning.'

Rose passed acquaintances by unnoticed as she jogged back to the flat in a dream. Her reception committee was waiting impatiently, as usual, demanding every last detail of the encounter.

'Wow,' said Fabia in awe. 'You're definitely winning, Rose.'

'But the prize is breakfast in a transport caff after slogging round the racetrack, not a candlelit dinner for two,' Rose reminded her, deliberately prosaic to hide her elation.

'Where Sinclair's concerned,' said Con, laughing, 'it probably counts for the same thing.'

When Rose arrived at the stadium next morning, sports bag in hand, Sinclair was racing round the track at a speed that exhausted her to watch.

'Hi,' he panted, coming to a stop beside her. 'Come on, a slow turn or two to warm up, then speed up a bit each circuit as you go along.'

When they took off round the track together Sinclair somehow managed to restrain his long stride to keep up with Rose as they ran, and to her surprise her technique improved so much with Sinclair for coach and pacemaker she even managed to stay upright when he called it a day at last and let her stop.

'Into the shower,' he ordered. 'Don't be long.'

Inside the deserted women's section Rose swathed her hair in a towel and leaned into a spray as hot as she could bear, then towelled herself hastily, slapped on some of the body lotion Fabia had provided, zipped up a yellow hooded sweatshirt and wriggled into the clinging jeans. Con had ordered her to use eyeshadow and mascara, but Rose was so eager to rejoin Sinclair she didn't bother. She loosened the braid, tied her hair back with a velvet ribbon and put some lipstick on as a gesture to the occasion. When she joined Sinclair outside her entire body simmered with excitement which increased when she saw the gleam of approval in his eyes.

'If you feel as good as you look,' he told her, taking her bag, 'the run was a success.'

'I feel great. And *very* hungry,' she added, almost dancing along beside him as they hurried down the hill to the town.

The transport café was packed, and full of steam and the smell of frying, and Rose loved every last thing about it. Sinclair exchanged greetings with some of the long-distance drivers who formed the majority of the clientele, seated Rose in a corner near the fogged window, then without consulting her went off to collect their meal.

'Bacon sandwiches—the staff of life,' he announced as he returned with the food.

Rose, who rarely ate any breakfast at all, fell on her sandwich ravenously. 'That was fabulous.' She sighed, as they drank strong tea afterwards. 'But if I lost any ounces on the track I've put them all back on now.'

'Is that why you run? To lose weight?' The assessing grey eyes scanned her from head to toe.

'No,' said Rose with complete truth. 'I just want to get fitter, release the endorphins and so on. Isn't that supposed to help the brain to function?'

'It does it for me,' he agreed. 'But it's part of my training. I should really have given up rugby for my finals' year, but the season will be over soon; then I'll channel all my energies into the last push to the exams.'

'No more running?' she said involuntarily.

Sinclair regarded her in silence for a moment. 'If I gave it up,' he said slowly, 'I think I'd miss my morning run. Now.'

Rose gulped down the last of her tea and stood up, afraid he'd tune in to her excitement if she stayed a second longer. 'Could I pay my share, please?'

'No.' Sinclair got up, smiling at her indulgently. 'You can pay next time.'

Next time! Rose's heart sang as she walked briskly up the hill with Sinclair, ignoring the awed, disbelieving looks of her peers as they recognised her companion. When they arrived at her entrance Rose thanked Sinclair for the meal and turned away quickly so he wouldn't suspect how much she longed to linger, but he caught her arm.

'Rose, wait a second. We've got another home match the day after tomorrow. Will you be there again?'

Again! So he had noticed her.

'I don't know. It depends,' she said vaguely.

To her delight he looked slightly put out. 'If not I'll be running on Sunday, same as usual. Come and try for an extra circuit and I'll buy you two bacon sandwiches this time to compensate.'

'OK,' she said casually, and forced herself take the stairs without a backward glance.

Con was full of admiration when she heard that Rose was neither turning up at the Saturday rugby game, nor going to the pub later on.

'Good move. Fabia's meeting Hargreaves at the Sceptre after the match, but I'll go to the flicks with you instead, Rose,' she added nobly.

'In the afternoon, if you like. The Cameo's showing one of those French films I'm supposed to like, so I'd

better see it to impress Sinclair. But in the evening you
have fun in the pub with Fabia and the others, as usual.
I shall stay here and watch TV. Or even do some work.'
Rose grinned, her eyes dancing.

'Clever little bunny! You don't need teacher any more.'

'I'm grateful for all the help I can get, but I do have
the odd idea of my own, Con. Sinclair let slip that he
noticed me at the match, and he definitely saw me at the
pub, so this week I shall be missing from both. But I need
you and Fabia and the rest there in force to make my
absence marked. And a detailed report when you get
back.'

During Saturday evening, while the comings and goings
outside early on made it difficult to concentrate on a
Shakespeare essay, Rose was almost sorry she'd had the
self-control to stay behind while the others went out. But,
quite apart from wanting Sinclair to note her absence, secretly Rose had worried that he might do no more than
give her a casual wave anyway, if she'd turned up at the
Sceptre. And no way was she willing to risk that.

'Sinclair was there, right enough,' said Con breathlessly, the moment she came through the door with Fabia.
'Flushed with victory, after his usual star turn on the
rugby pitch. He saw us arrive, *and* craned his neck to see
if you were with us. Then afterwards he kept glancing
over to our table to see if you'd put in a late appearance.
It's working, it's working!' She seized Rose's hands and
yanked her off the bed, whirling her round like a dervish
until they collapsed in a heap with Fabia, laughing their
heads off.

'What are you two *on*?' demanded Rose, giggling helplessly.

'Adrenaline,' gurgled Fabia, and eyed her with envy.

'Damn. I wish I'd drawn Sinclair's name out of the hat myself now.'

Con threw back her head with a yelp of laughter. 'Come *on*, Fabe, can you honestly see yourself pounding round the track at dawn?'

Fabia joined in the laughter good-naturedly. 'Not a chance. No man is worth that kind of effort.'

'I rather enjoy the running now,' confessed Rose. 'It gives a terrific buzz.'

'And ruins the mascara!'

'Never wear any.'

Con patted her hand. 'You don't need it, anyway. Is Sinclair still treating you like a kid, by the way?'

Rose thought it over. 'No,' she said slowly. 'I don't think he is.'

'I bet he's wondering where you are tonight, and who with,' said Fabia with relish. 'He'd never believe the truth.'

'He's about the only one who might,' said Con. 'Sinclair's got tunnel vision when it comes to the study bit, according to our faithful researchers. Will and Joe give off gamma rays of hero-worship whenever his name is mentioned.'

Rose felt a sharp twinge of conscience. 'I just hope he never finds out what we're up to.'

'He won't. Neither of them knows him well enough for intimate little chats. Besides, we have enough relevant information by now.' Con ticked off her fingers. 'Sinclair comes from somewhere near Edinburgh, lives in digs here in the town, likes foreign films and excels at almost every sport—as if we didn't know—but apparently he likes fishing, too, and holidays on Skye, and, of course, ambition is his middle name. There.'

'When did you find all this out?' demanded Rose.

'I had to be dangerously sweet to Hargreaves on the way home from the pub to wheedle the home background out of him.' Fabia batted her eyelashes. 'I stopped short of surrendering my virtue, but only just.'

'Good,' said Con approvingly. 'Keep him on the boil in case we need his help again. And don't even *try* to look noble—you know perfectly well you fancy him.'

'A good thing I do in the circumstances!' Fabia pulled a face. 'Though he's now convinced I've got a crush on our hero. Not that it matters. Will told me tonight I don't stand a chance in that direction, because Sinclair, I quote, "has no time to spare for girls".'

'Except at dawn's early light for Rose,' said Con, laughing.

CHAPTER THREE

NEXT morning Rose woke before the alarm went off, deeply depressed to find rain streaming down her window. Moving quietly to avoid disturbing the others, she got into her running gear, collected a yellow slicker from the hook behind the door, picked up her bag with the change of clothes, then shut herself in the bathroom for the rest of her preparations. She hurried out eventually into rain so heavy she was sure Sinclair wouldn't bother to turn up. But when she got to the stadium he was there before her, tall and faintly menacing in hooded black until his teeth showed white in the smile she was beginning to know so well.

'Hi. I didn't think you'd come.'

'I had my doubts,' she admitted, smiling cheerfully in response. She eyed the water-covered track with apprehension. 'Can we run on that?'

'I vote we don't in this weather.' He took her bag. 'I've got a suggestion.'

'Bacon sandwiches with no run for starters?' she said hopefully.

'Something like that. But there's a problem. The café doesn't open this early on Sundays.'

'Oh. Never mind,' said Rose, swallowing her disappointment. 'Some other time, then.'

'I live in digs in the town,' he said quickly, the faint trace of Scots in his accent more pronounced. 'And I make a great bacon sandwich. My landlady's away this weekend, babysitting, but she gives me the run of her kitchen.'

'Does she do that for all her boarders?'

'I'm her one and only.' His expression was hard to make out in the gloom. 'Will you join me for breakfast, Rose?'

Excitement swept through her like a tidal wave. 'Yes, I will. Thank you.'

He smiled. 'Come on, then, let's make a run for it. We've got a way to go before you get anything to eat.'

'And I thought I was let off for today!'

By the time they reached a crescent of solid Edwardian houses they were drenched. Sinclair unlocked the door of a house halfway along and hurried her into a mosaic-tiled hall, switched on lights and yanked off her dripping slicker.

'Take your shoes off,' he ordered, 'then go straight up the stairs to the bathroom and get into some dry clothes.'

'How about you?' She panted.

'I'll strip off in Mrs Bradley's bathroom down here— go on, hurry up. I'll start grilling the bacon while you change. My room's first on the right. Wait for me there.'

Wishing she could avoid getting sweaty and red-faced just once now and again in Sinclair's company, Rose stripped off her outer clothes in a blessedly warm bathroom, then pulled on dry socks, old, comfortable denims and an outsize baggy white sweater which grew larger every time she washed it. She dismantled her damp plait, rubbed her hair dry with her own towel, rather than mar the immaculate ones on the rail, used a hairbrush vigorously, then added the usual token touch of lipstick to her mouth and packed her wet things in the bag.

Rose felt like a trespasser when she ventured into Sinclair's room. There were piles of books everywhere. The sizeable table he used as a desk had obviously been cleared of them to make room for a large wooden tray set with tea-things, but books lay in stacks under it, and on shelves and on the floor either side of a big sofa. To her relief there was no bed. He obviously slept somewhere else. Through the rain sluicing down the big window at the back of the room Rose could see a drenched garden backing onto gardens in the street behind. Pleasant on a better day. And she envied him the room, which was three times the size of hers at the flat. She put her bag down and went to look at his books. Her aunt maintained that you could tell a lot about people from their taste in reading. But there was little to be learned from Sinclair's collection, which was all textbooks, bar a couple of volumes on fly fishing.

Rose turned guiltily as Sinclair came in with a platter of sandwiches. 'You were quick!' she exclaimed, hoping he couldn't tell how shy she felt now they were alone together.

Sinclair switched on a couple of lamps and plugged in a kettle. 'I put everything ready before I went out. I just had to light the grill and abracadabra, everything was ready in no time.' He handed her a length of kitchen paper in lieu of a napkin, and gave her a plate with two sandwiches on it, then made a pot of tea and sat down on a straight chair at the table and began to eat. Rose munched in silence for a lengthening interval, wishing she could think of something brilliantly clever to say.

'What's the matter, Rose?' he asked bluntly.

Her eyes met his with candour. 'I was just thinking that this isn't what I expected when I started out this morning.'

He raised an eyebrow. 'You'd prefer the transport café?'

'No, of course not.'

'Then don't look so scared. I'm perfectly harmless.'

She grinned involuntarily. 'So I've heard.'

He glared, his eyes suddenly wintry. 'And just what *have* you heard, little girl?' he drawled, ice in every word.

Rose blushed to the roots of her hair. 'Only that you're more interested in getting a double first than chasing after girls.'

His eyes softened. 'True enough. My surplus energies expend themselves on the track and the rugby pitch. The rest goes into this lot here.' He waved a hand at the encroaching books, then gave her the slow smile which made her insides dissolve. 'The rumours about my sexual preferences are false, by the way, in case you're wondering, spread in my first year by a female who resented my lack of interest.'

'I wasn't wondering,' she assured him blithely, and began on her second sandwich with more relish.

'Why not?'

Rose regarded him steadily. 'Because it's none of my business.'

Sinclair stared back in surprise. 'You're very blunt. Want some tea?'

'Yes, please.' He filled a beaker, added a splash of milk and handed it to her, pleasing Rose enormously because he'd remembered how she liked it.

'So you don't care whether I'm gay or not?' he demanded.

'No.' She shrugged. 'I fail to see why race, religion or sexual leanings should matter when it comes to friendship.'

Sinclair leaned forward, his hands clasped between his knees as he peered down into her face. 'You really mean that, don't you?'

'Yes.' Rose gave him a crooked little smile. 'Wet behind the ears I may be in your eyes, but I have my beliefs.'

'Your parents fostered them?'

Her face shadowed. 'They began the process, but they died when I was fourteen. I live with my aunt. Minerva holds strong views on everything, so I suppose I've taken some of them on board myself without even realising it.'

Sinclair got up, seeming taller than usual to Rose from her seat on his sofa. He took her mug and plate from her and put them on the tray, then to her astonishment he sat beside her and took her hand.

'Would you like to tell me about your parents?' he said gently.

Rose gave him a startled, sidelong glance, deeply conscious of the hard, warm hand grasping hers. Then after a moment's hesitation she told him about the joyrider who'd put an end to her parents' lives one afternoon on a narrow country road in Warwickshire.

'They were on their way to fetch me from school.' Rose bit her lip. 'For a long time I just couldn't accept that they were gone, even after I went to live with my aunt. Minerva owns a bookshop in a small town in the Cotswolds, and after—after the accident I moved into the flat over the shop with her.'

'Poor little kid,' said James quietly. 'It must have been tough for you.'

'I won't pretend it wasn't. But I've been fortunate, too. My father was a lot older than Minerva, so I look on her more as friend than aunt now I'm older. And I still have my memories of a happy childhood, and the holidays I spent with Mother and Dad.' Feeling horribly guilty, she recalled herself to the matter in hand. 'We even went to Scotland once, to Skye.' The last bit, a vital part of Con's strategy, was her first real lie, and she gulped down some tea to cover the rush of guilty colour to her face.

'Skye!' exclaimed Sinclair. 'When my father was alive

we went there once a year. I love it there. How about you?'

'I don't remember much about it. I was quite young, and it rained a lot,' said Rose, deliberately vague. 'My father went fishing, and Mother and I visited woollen mills.'

'Did your father do much fishing?' he asked with interest.

'Yes. When he could. Trout, like you.' She went cold for a moment. 'I saw the books on your shelves,' she said hurriedly, and went on talking to cover her blunder. 'Dad made the most beautiful flies. He'd sit with a special little vice at the kitchen table, listening to opera tapes while he created tiny works of art. I still have some of them. The fishing flies, I mean. His rods were sold.'

The grasp tightened. 'You still miss him.'

'I miss them both.' Rose hesitated. 'But it comforts me to know that they're together.'

'You really believe that?'

'Yes.' Her chin lifted. 'Because I need to believe it.'

There was silence between them for a while.

'My father died when I was twelve,' said Sinclair abruptly.

Rose sat perfectly still, hardly daring to breathe. In her wildest dreams she'd never imagined he'd confide in her in return.

'He died in his sleep,' he went on. 'When my mother woke up one morning he was just—gone. Dad was a workaholic with a heart problem. Fatal combination.'

'I'm sorry.' Rose tightened her fingers in sympathy.

'When I was eighteen my mother married again. He's a good man, and they're happy together. But...' he paused.

'You feel left out?'

He frowned thoughtfully. 'I've never thought of it in quite those terms, but, yes, I suppose I do. That's why I applied for a college down here. I could have gone to Edinburgh or St Andrews, but I opted to get right away to leave the newlyweds in peace. I even took off for a year between school and college. Went backpacking round Australia.'

'Sounds wonderful. I've never done anything adventurous like that,' said Rose enviously. 'Do you mind? That your mother remarried, I mean?' Then she held her breath, afraid she'd trespassed.

But Sinclair shook his head. 'No. I don't mind at all. She waited until I was ready to leave home, though Donald would have married her long before then from choice. My mother was only fortyish when they finally tied the knot. And even in a son's eyes a very attractive lady.' He gave her a wry look. 'Donald's a successful advocate, and a very self-contained sort of bloke, but it was obvious, even to me, that he was mad about my mother from the moment he met her. Still is. Mother sold our home when she moved in with him. His house is a big, rambling place, and there's a room in it kept solely for me, but I can't help feeling like a visitor there—' He stopped dead, shaking his head.

'What's the matter?'

'I can't believe I'm telling you all this stuff. I don't usually bore people rigid with my life history.' He squeezed her hand. 'You must be a very good listener, young Rose.'

Now, she thought reluctantly, would be a good time to leave. She detached her hand gently and got up. 'I'd better leave you to your books. Thank you for breakfast, and— and for talking to me.'

Sinclair got to his feet and stretched, suddenly so overpoweringly male in the small room Rose felt a sudden urge to run, like an animal scenting danger.

'The average man doesn't need much persuading to talk about himself,' he said wryly.

'Average' was the last word Rose would have applied to Sinclair. 'I must go—or should I help you wash up first?'

He ruffled her hair, smiling. Like petting a puppy, she thought, resigned.

'I've got a better idea. Stay and have some more tea. It's still hissing down out there.'

Rose glanced at the window. 'You're right. OK. Then I really must get back.'

'Rose, it's only half-eight, and it's Sunday. What's the rush?'

'I must be keeping you from your work.'

'I've got the rest of the day for that.' His eyes narrowed. 'Or is there someone waiting for you?'

He didn't like the idea!

'A playmate of my own age, you mean?' she said, smiling.

'Hell, Rose, you're not *that* much younger than me,' he said irritably, and raised an eyebrow. '*Is* there someone?'

Afraid he might wash his hands of her if she even hinted there might be, Rose shook her head. 'No. Only my flatmates. And I doubt if they're even awake yet.'

'Right.' He picked up the kettle. 'You sit there for a minute, and I'll go and fill this again.'

'Can't I wash the plates, or something?'

'I'll let you off as it's your first visit. Next time you can do the catering.'

Next time! Rose sat deep in thought after he'd gone. It seemed Con might be right. It actually *was* possible to deliberately rouse a man's interest. Though it was impossible to imagine James Sinclair as any woman's slave. Nor falling madly in love with Rose Dryden, either, however faithfully she followed the plan of campaign. But he was definitely taken with her a little bit. Enough to invite her back here, and coach her on the track. Which was way beyond anything she'd expected.

When Sinclair came back he gave her a searching look as he plugged in the kettle. 'Where were you last night, Rose?'

'Working.'

He frowned. 'A part-time job? Where?'

'No job. I was writing an essay. I went to the Cameo in the afternoon, then caught up with some work afterwards. Why?'

'I noticed you weren't in the pub. I wondered if you were ill.' He made two more beakers of tea, and handed her one.

She shook her head, full of secret jubilation. 'Since I've taken up running again I'm fighting fit.'

'I said you would be. So what film did you see?'

'They were showing a re-run of *Manon des Sources*. It's one of my favourites,' she added, crossing mental fingers.

His eyes lit up with enthusiasm. 'Mine too. I never managed to catch the prequel—what was it called?'

'*Jean de Florette*. That's on this week for three days— then it's *Belle du Jour*,' Rose added hastily, afraid she'd been too obvious. She sighed. 'Catherine Deneuve is so beautiful.'

Sinclair shrugged. 'Not my type. I prefer my women dark.'

'Sounds as though you own a harem,' said Rose flippantly, and drained her mug to avoid looking at him.

'Your face is very expressive, Rose,' he teased. 'What are you thinking?'

'I just wondered if you had someone—a girl, I mean—back home. Which is absolutely none of my business, of course,' she added in a rush, wishing she'd held her tongue.

'I don't have a woman back home, or anywhere else for that matter. The grapevine is absolutely accurate,' he said mockingly. 'I've got no time for girls.'

'Which is a cue for this one to leave, if ever I heard one,' she said promptly, and jumped to her feet. 'Rain or no rain, it's time I was off.'

He ran down the stairs ahead of her to fetch her shoes and slicker. 'Shall I call a cab?'

'No. The exercise will do me good.'

'Hands up.' He put the slicker over her head, then drew the hood over her hair. 'See you on the track in the morning, then.'

Rose smiled non-committally as she stamped her feet into her damp track shoes. 'Thanks again for my breakfast,' she said, when he opened the front door. 'Goodbye.'

'Goodbye, *James*,' he corrected.

'Everyone else calls you Sinclair,' she pointed out, careful to pronounce it as he did.

'Exactly.'

Rose smiled uncertainly. 'Goodbye, then—James.'

'See you in the morning. Don't hang about on the way back, and straight in the shower when you get there.'

She saluted smartly, gave him a cheeky grin, then took her bag from him and went off down the path at speed, turning to wave at him as he stood at the open door.

When she arrived at the flat, sodden, out of breath, and utterly triumphant, she dumped the dripping slicker in the bathroom, then went to join Con and Fabia.

'Where on earth have you been until now?' demanded Con.

Fabia eyed Rose's glowing face with suspicion. 'You can't have been racing round that track all this time!'

'No, I haven't.' Rose began stuffing her shoes with kitchen paper to dry them out. 'There was so much surface water James said it was unsafe to run so he took me back to his digs for breakfast.' She looked up, laughing at the identical look on both faces.

'At his digs?' said Con faintly. 'Like in his *room*?'

Rose nodded gleefully. 'His landlady was away for the weekend, and he's the only lodger. We had the house to ourselves.'

Fabia blew out her cheeks and sat down abruptly. 'You've cracked it, then!'

'Hold on. I haven't achieved that much,' warned Rose. 'James isn't in love with me—'

'Not yet,' put in Con, eyes gleaming, 'but he's interested enough to ask you back to his place for breakfast.'

'For which I was truly thankful,' said Rose piously. 'I think my efforts on the track entitled me to a couple of bacon sandwiches at the very least.'

'Did you have to make them?'

'No. *James*,' she said with emphasis, 'made them with his own fair hands.'

'Did he ask you to call him that?' demanded Con, impressed.

'Yes. Sinclair to everyone else; James to me.'

'So what happens next?' said Fabia eagerly. 'Has he asked you for a proper date?'

Rose's face fell. 'No. Though heaven knows I hinted enough—told him about the film we saw, and the one showing this week. He may like foreign films, but he's not taking me to see one.'

'Never mind. I think you've worked miracles as it is,' consoled Con. 'When do you see him again?'

'He said he'd see me at the track in the morning, but I suppose I'd better give it a miss until Tuesday.'

Con shook her head. 'If he wants to see you tomorrow, be there.'

'Won't that be overkill?'

'No. This, my pet, is phase three. Time to hot things up.'

'I just hope it doesn't end in tears!'

Fabia frowned. 'Why should it? It's just a game.'

Rose thought about that a lot later that night, once she was in bed. Since the exchange of confidences with James it no longer felt like a game. Which lay on her conscience so heavily sleep was elusive. But next morning she got up early, just the same, and let herself out into a cold, but thankfully dry morning to join James at the stadium, smiling in welcome.

'Hi! I've done my bit,' he informed her. 'Ready to try for an extra lap today?'

Rose nodded eagerly, went through a few warming-up exercises, then set off with him round the track. Under his tuition she found herself running a slightly faster circuit every time, exhilarated by her success, until halfway round for the fourth a sudden, stinging pain in her foot ruined her balance and she fell heavily, her momentum sending her rolling over and over to land flat on her back, completely winded.

'Rose!' James fell on his knees beside her. 'What the hell happened? Are you all right?'

Rose had no breath to spare for talking. While she fought to get air in her lungs he ran his hands over her arms and legs, probed her ankles, found nothing broken and pulled her carefully to her feet.

'Come on, breathe. Deep, even breaths. That's the way. Good girl. Lean against me for a bit.'

Rose obeyed gratefully, heaving in gulps of air, but soon grew much too conscious of the heat and scent of his body, the heart beating like a drum against her cheek. She pulled away, smiling shakily. 'Stupid—thing—to do. Sorry.'

'There must have been water on the track,' said James gruffly. 'Are you sure you're all right?'

She nodded. 'Embarrassed, that's all.'

'Here, take my arm. I'll help you back to the flat.'

Rose stared at him, horrified. 'No, please! You don't need to. I'll be fine.'

He scowled down at her. 'Be sensible, Rose, you're limping.'

'There's something in my shoe.'

James sat her down on the track and removed the shoe, swearing under his breath when he found a small nail sticking up inside it. He removed her bloodstained sock and located a puncture on the sole of her foot. 'No wonder you fell, Rose. What the hell was something like this doing on the track?'

'Maybe it got washed down from somewhere in that weather yesterday.'

'In which case there may be more. I'd better report it. In the meantime you need a dressing. Wait there a minute. I'll raid the first-aid box in the men's showers.'

While he was gone one of his rugby team mates appeared for a morning run, and hurried to Rose in surprise.

'What's wrong, love? Sprained your ankle?' said the large, amiable giant.

'No, I trod on a nail,' she confessed, feeling horribly self-conscious.

'Bad luck! I'll get you something to put on your foot,' he offered, then stared in astonishment as James appeared.

'Sinclair? A bit late in the day for you, isn't it?'

'Hi, Greg. Be careful on the track. There may be more like this.' James held up the nail he'd taken from Rose's shoe.

Greg looked on, riveted, as a sticking plaster was applied to Rose's foot and her sock and shoe carefully replaced.

'There,' said James, pulling her to her feet. 'Can you stand on it, Rose?'

She tried the foot gingerly. It was sore, but she could walk. 'It's fine,' she said firmly. 'Sorry for all the fuss.' She gave a smile that encompassed both men. 'Thanks a lot. I'd better get back. Bye.'

'Look, I could easily carry a little thing like you back to campus,' said Greg, with enthusiasm which evaporated as he met Sinclair's ferocious glare.

'It's very kind of you, but I can manage. Really.' Rose limped rapidly from the stadium in embarrassment, her morning utterly ruined.

When she got back to the flat the others were still in bed. Rose went off for a shower, choking back a sob as she dried herself. It had ended in tears after all. Because there'd be no more running for a bit. And no hope of seeing James again until she could.

Fabia burst in suddenly, scaring Rose to death. '*Run*— phone call.'

Wrapping herself in a towel as she ran, Rose flew to the sitting room, afraid something had happened to her aunt. 'Hello?' she gasped into the phone.

'Rose? James.'

Her eyebrows shot to her hair. When she nodded silently in answer to the incredulous question in Con's eyes her friend gave a triumphant thumbs-up sign, and whisked herself from the room.

'Hi,' Rose answered, when she had herself in hand.

'I wanted to make sure you got back in one piece. How's the foot?'

'OK. The nail wasn't big enough to go in very far.'

'Good. But you'd better not run on it for a while.'

'No.'

There was a pause.

'Rose.'

'Yes?'

'You took off so suddenly I didn't have a chance to ask just now.' This time the pause stretched Rose's nerves to breaking point. 'Are you doing anything tonight?' James asked at last.

Rose clamped her teeth together to stop them chattering. 'No,' she said after a pause of her own, hoping he thought she'd been leafing through her diary.

'The French film you mentioned—' He paused.

'Jean de Florette?'

'Right. I thought we might see it together.'

'OK,' she said, hoping she sounded casual.

'Good. I'll pick you up outside the flat at seven.'

'No need to come out of your way,' she said quickly. 'I can meet you at the Cameo.'

'You can't walk down here on that foot, Rose. I'll fetch you in the car.'

Car?

'See you later, then.' She put the phone down in a dream.

'What did he want?' demanded Con, rushing in.

Rose turned dazed eyes on her friend. 'He's taking me to the Cameo tonight. In someone's car.'

'Fabia,' yelled Con in triumph. 'Get your self in here. Phase three is up and running!'

CHAPTER FOUR

ROSE came back to the present with an effort, annoyed to find she'd been daydreaming so long the bath water was cold and so was she. With no time to iron her original choice for the evening, she pulled on a black jersey dress with a long skirt slit to to the knee, and swiftly brushed the thick, glossy hair which these days stopped short just above her shoulders. She did her face with swift, practised skill Fabia Hargreaves would have been proud of, and as the finishing touch sprayed herself with perfume and slid her feet into low-heeled black suede shoes. Because Anthony Garrett was very conscious of his height, which at best could only be described as medium, Rose left her high heels at home when she went out with him.

On normal Saturdays Anthony usually arrived in Chastlecombe long before she closed the shop, and arrived to collect her punctually at eight. But by the time he rang her private doorbell that night he was almost an hour late.

'Traffic bad, Anthony?' said Rose, as they went upstairs. 'Have a drink.'

'Thanks. You're an angel.' He dumped a suitcase down, then slumped on Rose's sofa with a sigh, looking tired, and consequently every year of his age for once. 'Sorry I'm late. My blasted phone had run out of juice, so I couldn't let you know I was held up by an accident. The Friday traffic was bad enough before then, but I've been crawling along for the past hour.' He accepted the whisky gratefully and tossed it back in one swallow. 'I needed that.' He smiled up at her in appreciation. 'You look wonderful, Rose.'

'Thank you, kind sir. I rang the restaurant to say we were delayed, by the way, but they're holding the table. Not,' she added, 'without reluctance.'

Anthony frowned. 'Why? We eat there often enough.'

'It's Valentine's night.'

He clapped a hand to his forehead and groaned. 'Hell and damnation—I meant to buy you some flowers, but I forgot. My apologies again, Rose.'

Her eyes narrowed thoughtfully. 'In that case, Anthony, I take it you didn't send me that card over there, either.'

He eyed the card with unmistakable hostility. 'No, I damn well did not. Who did?'

'No idea.' Rose went into the kitchen to fetch the rose. 'This arrived, too.'

Anthony jumped to his feet, scowling. 'Your old pal Mark Cummings, I suppose.'

So he hadn't sent the rose, either.

'I have no idea,' Rose assured him. 'We really ought to get going, Anthony.'

'Yes, of course.' He looked down at his rumpled suit with distaste. 'Look, could I have a swift shower and change? I was too late to get to the King's Head first.'

Rose had been wondering about the suitcase. She waved him off to the bathroom, then stared down at the card again. If Anthony hadn't sent it—not that she thought he had—who *was* her unknown admirer? If it was the joker with the heavy breathing the idea was so disturbing Rose found it an effort, later, to be bright, animated company over dinner in a restaurant which had pulled out all the stops for Valentine's night. Anthony, smart in a new suit, did his best to make up for his late arrival, and ordered expensive wine to go with the meal. But when they reached the coffee stage he downed his accompanying cognac with uncharacteristic speed.

'Rose,' he said, leaning forward to avoid being overheard. 'There's something I want to ask.' His eyes, still bloodshot from driving, locked with hers with an intensity which made her apprehensive.

'In that case,' she said lightly, 'let's go back to the flat. There's too much noise here.'

It was only a short walk back to the cobbled arcade where Dryden Books rubbed shoulders with shops which sold antiques and expensive clothes. But because Anthony made no attempt to talk on the way Rose felt on edge by the time she unlocked the private door alongside her double-fronted shop.

'Coffee?' she said brightly, when they reached the flat.

'Not for the moment. Come and sit down.' He took her hand and drew her down beside him on the sofa. 'Look, Rose, we've been seeing each other on a regular basis for some time now,' he began.

'An occasional Saturday evening over the past month or two,' she amended quickly, not liking the sound of this.

'Almost three months,' he corrected. 'More than long enough for me to know my own mind, and, hopefully, yours.'

Rose eyed him warily. 'What's this leading to, Anthony?'

'Surely you can recognise a proposal when you hear one! I'm asking you to marry me,' he said, and tried to kiss her, but she dodged away and went to sit in a nearby chair.

'Why?' she asked quietly.

'*Why?*' Anthony stared at her, affronted. 'Because I care for you, of course, and I believe we could be happy together. Don't you enjoy time spent with me?'

'Well, yes. But I had no idea you were thinking about marriage.' Rose raised an eyebrow. 'Tell me the truth, Anthony. Isn't this sudden talk of marriage just a deep-seated need to show your ex-wife you can attract a younger woman?'

'That's unfair!' Colour flooded into Anthony's face, then receded again, leaving him pale. 'In the beginning there was an element of that,' he admitted at last, gaining her respect. 'But it soon changed into something very different. When I saw that stupid card earlier I felt so jealous it stampeded me into wanting to make our relationship official.' He looked at her in appeal. 'Will you at least consider the idea of marrying me, Rose?'

'I don't think so,' she said gently.

Anthony jumped to his feet, so obviously thunderstruck by her refusal he couldn't sit still. 'Why not?' he demanded. 'Is there someone else?'

Rose sighed. 'Not in the way you mean.'

'What other way is there?' he shot at her, pacing up and down. 'I suppose it's Mark Cummings. Your old pal with his sob story. Do you really want to tie yourself to a man with a failed marriage and a child—' He stopped dead.

'Both of those things apply to you, Anthony,' she pointed out.

'That's different,' he said, discomfited. 'I'm legally divorced, at least, and Marcus is a teenager, not a toddler like the Cummings child.'

Rose nodded. 'Nevertheless, any marriage between you and me, Anthony, would present certain problems.'

'If you mean Marcus, I don't foresee any trouble there. He wouldn't be living with us. Besides, he likes you, Rose.'

'Good. I'm glad.' She eyed him questioningly. 'But if,

by any chance, I did consider marrying you, where would you expect me to live?'

He frowned, taken aback. 'Why, with me, naturally.'

'In London?'

'Is that a problem?'

'It's certainly could be. My life is here in Chastlecombe now, with friends and familiar faces round me, and a livelihood which gives me pleasure. And independence.' Rose hesitated, then decided to tell him the truth. 'But the major obstacle between us is a secret from my past.'

Anthony's eyes narrowed. 'A secret?'

Rose nodded, glancing involuntarily at the rose. 'Yes.'

'Are you talking about a lover?'

She nodded. 'Or to be more accurate, the consequences of having a lover.'

He swallowed convulsively. 'You mean you had a child?'

'No, Anthony.'

'Then, what *is* this mysterious problem?'

She turned away wearily. 'I can't marry anyone at this moment in time, Anthony, because I'm still married to someone else.'

'What!' He spun her round, his face dark with anger. 'And you've never seen fit to tell me?'

Rose lifted her chin with sudden hauteur. 'I've never told anyone. Ever. Not even Minerva. I wouldn't have told *you*, believe me, if you hadn't talked of marriage.'

'What else did you think I had in mind at my age!' he demanded furiously. 'I'm too old to be your boyfriend—'

'I think the word's "partner" these days.'

'Partner implies a hell of a sight more privileges than I enjoy,' he snapped. 'And now I discover there's a whole area of your life I knew nothing about.'

'Why should you? It's my business entirely, Anthony. But if it's any consolation, no one else knows, either.'

'Aren't you forgetting someone?' he demanded. 'This mysterious husband of yours?'

Rose's lips tightened. 'Of course I haven't forgotten him.'

Anthony threw out his hands. 'Then what's the problem? Won't he agree to a divorce?'

'I don't know.'

'You don't *know*? Why the hell not?'

'I've never asked him.'

Anthony exerted control with visible effort. 'Rose,' he said at last. 'How old were you when you got married?'

'Eighteen.'

He stared at her incredulously. 'Ten years ago?'

'Yes.'

'Then why in heaven's name haven't you got round to a divorce?'

'Because our parting was so hostile I swore he'd be the one to ask first,' said Rose with passion.

'Why hasn't he?'

'No idea. It certainly wouldn't have cost him financially.' Her mouth tightened. 'I wouldn't have touched a penny of his.'

Anthony eyed her thoughtfully. 'It sounds to me, Rose, as though you need to be free of this man, regardless of your intentions towards *me*.'

'You could be right.'

'Can you tell me about it?'

Her face shuttered. 'I'd rather not discuss it.'

'Whatever you say, Rose.' He hesitated. 'Just answer one question, then I'll go. Did you leave this man, or was it the other way about?'

'I left him.'

'Not that it matters, after all this time.' Anthony gave her a bleak smile. 'As you well know, I'm clued up about divorce. Mine, due to Marcus and the house, was more complicated. But are you aware that after ten years apart the court will grant you a divorce whether your husband agrees to it or not?'

'Really?' Rose frowned. 'Then it's strange that he's never got round to divorcing *me*. Perhaps he has and forgot to notify me.' She shrugged. 'Or maybe he's just forgotten he was ever married to me.'

Anthony shook his head, looked depressed. 'No man could forget he'd been married to *you*, Rose.'

When she was alone at last Rose was amazed to find it was still a few minutes short of twelve, the time Anthony always left her. As far as the world knew, or cared, he could have been making mad, passionate love to her in the interval between dining together and his departure every time they met, but Anthony Garrett, deeply conventional at heart, always returned to the King's Head before midnight. And until tonight had never attempted to put their relationship on a more intimate basis. For which she'd been grateful. She liked his company well enough in small doses, but there was nothing sexual in their relationship. On her side, at least. Nor did she mourn the lack. She'd been through all that before, and it had never turned out well for her.

It could have been two in the morning by the way she felt when Rose got ready for bed. Desperate for sleep after the emotional drain of the past hour, she was about to switch off her light when her bedside phone rang. Thinking it might be Bel, to say she couldn't get in next day, Rose picked up the receiver, then almost dropped it again when someone whispered her name and rang off. Hand shaking, she pressed buttons frantically, but the number had again been withheld.

Trembling, and this time more frightened than she cared to admit, Rose pulled on her dressing gown and went to make herself some tea, then took it back to bed and sat propped up against all her pillows with the lights on, feeling furious as well as frightened. Just minutes ago she'd been struggling to keep awake long enough to get to bed, but the phone call had changed all that. Speculation on the identity of her caller would do no good at all. Probably give her nightmares. Rose sighed, resigned. There was one infallible way to occupy her mind, of course. Talking about her marriage to Anthony had brought it all back in full force. And perhaps this was a good thing. If she recalled the past so that every aspect of it was clear in her mind, it might make things easier when she broached the subject of divorce. As she should have done long since.

CHAPTER FIVE

ROSE had forced herself to walk downstairs sedately for her first real date with James Sinclair. Refusing all offers of help from Con and Fabia, she'd worn her own clothes, made up her own face, and tied her hair back with a scarf in preference to anything more elaborate. But because none of this took very much time she was ready and waiting far too soon, and felt almost sick with suspense by the time James rang their bell to say he was waiting downstairs.

Waved off by her friends as though she were going away on honeymoon, Rose found James leaning against an elderly sports car.

'Hi,' she said breathlessly. 'Nice wheels.'

He patted the bonnet possessively. 'She's been out of commission for a while, waiting for spare parts. I've just got her back from the garage.' He held the door for her. 'I put the hood up to make sure you stay dry for once tonight.'

Knowing that Con and Fabia were glued to the window two floors up, watching them as they left, Rose huddled down in the bucket seat, simmering with the secret excitement that affected her from time to time in present company.

'How's the foot?' James asked. 'No infection?'

'No. It's fine. A bit sore, but I'll live.'

The lights had already gone down at the Cameo before they arrived. Once they were seated in the dark together Rose sat perfectly still, staring at the screen, hardly able to believe this was happening. Gradually her excitement subsided, allowing her to translate the subtitles sufficiently well to follow the plot. If James discussed it afterwards, she reminded herself, the so-called fan of foreign-language movies had better be able to make intelligent responses.

When the film was over they went outside to find rain coming down in sheets again.

'Can you run for the car on that foot, or shall I carry you?' James asked as they stood in the foyer.

'I can run,' she assured him, and he took her hand and raced with her to the car.

'It's early,' he said as he drove off. 'Fancy a drink and a sandwich?'

Did she!

'Yes, please,' said Rose with enthusiasm.

'We could go to a pub, or you could come back to my place again, if you like,' he said casually.

'Your place,' she said promptly. By some miracle they hadn't seen anyone from college at the cinema, but it might be a different story if they went to a pub in the town. And Rose couldn't endure the thought of other people watching them, speculating on their relationship. Which wasn't a relationship, really. Not yet.

When they arrived outside the familiar house the door flew open as James hurried Rose towards it, revealing an elderly lady with grey curly hair and a beaming smile of welcome.

'I heard the car,' she explained. 'Come in quickly out of that rain. Now then, James, introduce me.'

'Mrs Bradley this is Rose. Rose Dryden. She's a student up at the college.'

'How nice to meet you, my dear. Let me take that wet coat.'

Rose murmured something polite, and obediently surrendered her jacket, feeling a little shy as James's landlady cast an approving eye over her.

'We decided on coffee and a sandwich here instead of a pub, Mrs B,' said James, smiling.

'I should think so, too, the prices they charge. There's some ham in the fridge, James, and cheese and salad greens. Take what you want.' Mrs Bradley gave them a motherly smile. 'I'll leave you to it, and get back to my television.'

James took Rose into the immaculate, modernised kitchen at the end of the hall and handed her a loaf. 'Can you cut bread?'

'Not unless you want doorsteps. You slice, I'll butter and fill.'

'Done.' He ruffled her hair indulgently, then took a selection of sandwich ingredients from the fridge and laid them out on the counter. 'No bacon tonight.'

'Which of this lot do you fancy?'

'Everything.'

While they discussed the film Rose assembled thin wafers of ham and cheese, watercress, chives and two varieties of lettuce, used some dressing she found in the fridge, then fastened the creations together with toothpicks James produced from a cupboard.

When she'd finished Rose wasn't given long to wonder where they were expected to eat. James put the platter of sandwiches on a tray, added a couple of plates, some linen napkins provided by his landlady for the occasion, then told Rose to go upstairs ahead of him to his room.

So Mrs Bradley had no objection to female visitors.

James eyed his guest closely as he switched on lamps. 'What's the matter, Rose? Would you prefer to eat down in the kitchen?'

'Is that what you normally do?'

'No. Apart from the Sunday roast I fetch my meals up here on a tray.' He shook his head in mock reproof. 'Stop worrying, Rose. You look good enough to eat, it's true, but I promise I'll restrict myself to the sandwiches. You could have chosen the pub instead of coming here,' he pointed out.

Crimson-faced, but comforted by the thought that at least she wasn't sweaty with it for once, Rose smiled at him in contrition. 'Sorry. I was just wondering about your Mrs Bradley's views on female visitors.'

'Pleased as Punch when I warned her that I might be bringing you back tonight. Apparently she thinks it high time I had a "nice young lady".' He put a sandwich on a plate and handed it to her. 'Surely you've been in some other guy's room on campus?'

'Yes, but not on my own.'

James waved her to the sofa and sat down beside her to eat. 'I can't believe one of those hopefuls buzzing round you hasn't asked you out.'

Rose nodded, mouth full.

'Did you go?'

'No.'

'Why not?'

Rose glared at him. 'You ask a lot of questions!'

James grinned. 'Sorry, sorry. Just interested.'

'Edgy, you mean, because I said yes to you but refused the others,' she said bluntly.

He threw back his head and laughed. 'Straight between the eyes!'

Rose went on with her sandwich, then gave him a side-long look as he sobered. 'I suppose it's my turn to say "stop worrying", now.'

'I'm not worried,' he assured her. 'But I can't help wondering why I got lucky when the others didn't.'

Rose bristled. 'Unlike you, they don't share my taste in films.' Then, casting caution to the winds she said, 'And now you've brought the subject up, James Sinclair, your interest in girls is so famously non-existent how come *I* "got lucky", as you so charmingly put it.'

'Ouch—the rose has thorns!' James gave her a very straight look. 'Because you're different. No artifice, no tricks. Not like a girl at all, in fact.'

No tricks! Rose burned with guilt. 'I'm a very normal sort of female,' she warned him.

'Don't think I hadn't noticed,' he said dryly, and got up. 'Which would you like, tea, coffee or beer?'

'Tea, please.' She pulled a face. 'I drink lager when I go out, but I don't really like it.'

James wagged a finger at her. 'Then don't drink it, for Pete's sake. Go for mineral water or fruit juice.'

'It seems so childish!'

He smiled as he made the tea. 'What does that matter, Rose? Be yourself. And remember,' he added, 'it's a great advantage for a girl with your looks to keep a clear head when the men you're with are drinking.'

'True,' she conceded, elated by the casual compliment, 'but the ones I know best are a *fairly* temperate bunch— most of them too broke to drink all that much, anyway.'

'But there's a Valentine dance in the union shortly. If you're going, take care. It's been a pretty rowdy occasion in the past,' he warned, and handed her a mug of tea. 'You haven't finished your sandwich.'

'Give me time.'

James sat down beside her, patting her knee. 'Are we friends again, then?'

'Of course we are,' she said cheerfully. 'Can't alienate my coach!'

He eyed her askance. 'Is *that* how you think of me?'

'Not entirely.' Rose munched deliberately for a while before giving him a demure little smile. 'You've been so kind to me I suppose I look on you as a sort of older brother.'

James spluttered violently, spilled some scalding tea in his lap and leapt up with a howl.

Rose jumped up to dab him down with Mrs Bradley's linen napkin, but with a choked sound he thrust her hands away and raced from the room. She stared after him blankly, then sat down again to drink tea until James came back, wearing battered old cords.

Rose eyed him warily. 'Are you all right?'

'Yes. My jeans suffered the most—I'd just washed the damn things, too.' He sat down again, arms folded, his straight black brows drawn together in a heavy frown. After a while he turned towards her, and took her hand. 'Look, Rose, I think we'd better have a little talk.'

She stiffened. Had he got wind of the plan somehow? 'What about?'

To her surprise he shifted uneasily, his eyes glued to their clasped hands. 'Look, from what you told me I take it there hasn't been much of a male presence in your life, right?'

Rose relaxed a little. 'Right.'

'This aunt you live with, does she have any male friends?'

'Yes, several,' she said, surprised. 'Minerva goes out quite a lot. Dinner, concerts, that kind of thing.'

'But I assume you went to a girls' school?' he went on doggedly.

'Yes, I did. What *is* this?'

'Bear with me. Did you know any boys?'

'Of course I did. Blokes from the neighboring school. One of them was even my boyfriend at one time—brother of my best friend, Bel.'

He relaxed a little. 'Nice lad?'

'Mark's very nice indeed.' Rose turned dancing eyes on him. 'James, I do know about the birds and the bees, if that's where this is leading.'

'I'm sure you do. But in my opinion you need a bit of advice from the male point of view.' He cleared his throat, still staring down at their hands. 'Rose, are you a virgin?'

She tore her hand away and jumped up, her eyes blazing. 'What business is that of yours?'

James leapt to bar her way to the door.

'Out of my way!' she ordered furiously. 'I'm going.'

'Calm *down*, Rose. Let me explain. I can't help worrying about you.'

'Well, you needn't,' she snapped. 'I can take care of myself.'

He thrust his hands through his mop of dark hair. 'Hell, this is embarrassing. Listen! Why do you think I rushed out of the room just now?'

Rose simmered down a little. 'Because you spilt your tea, of course.'

James smiled ruefully. 'That was part of it. But the main reason was my—er, response when you touched me in that particular danger zone. You just can't do that kind of thing. Oh, God, now you've gone red again. Does it help that I'm hot under the collar, too?'

Rose didn't know whether to laugh or cry. So she laughed. And James laughed with her, relieved, and caught her in a hug.

'Promise me you won't do that with anyone else!' he ordered.

That was an easy one.

'I promise.' She gasped, her eyes dancing as they met his. 'And just so you won't stay awake all night wondering, I am.'

'You're what?' he said huskily.

'What you said.'

Suddenly neither of them was laughing any more. Rose tensed as she saw the grey eyes narrow to a gleam which rang alarm bells in her head. But she couldn't have moved to save her life. Time seemed to stop as James slowly bent his head to hers. When he kissed her at last the touch of his lips on hers was gentle enough, but it triggered a response that swept through them both like a bush fire. He pulled her close and kissed her again, no longer gentle, and she leaned into him, her lips parting in welcome to his tongue, and instantly both of them were breathing harder than at any time on the track. James picked her up and sat down with her on his lap, his mouth moving over her face, feature by feature, as he undid the scarf to run his hands through her hair.

'This wasn't supposed to happen,' he whispered.

'I know,' she said breathlessly. 'You've got no time for girls.'

'Other girls,' he corrected, and kissed her with renewed heat.

Rose, in seventh heaven, thrust guilt from her mind and gave herself up to the utter joy of James's lips on hers and his body hard and hot against her own as he fought to restrict himself to kisses. She realised, deeply touched, that he was gripping her waist tight to prevent his hands moving higher, and returned his kisses with such wanton fervour by way of appreciation he broke away at last and sat with his head in his hands, breathing raggedly.

'I swear I didn't bring you here for this,' he said hoarsely.

Rose, speechless for a variety of reasons, put out a hand to touch his. He seized it without looking at her.

'Are you all right?' he asked eventually.

'Yes,' she managed.

James turned with a questioning look which made Rose conscious of hair all over the place and a mouth that felt swollen. 'Has that happened before to you?' he asked harshly.

She pretended to misunderstand. 'I've been kissed enough. But never like that.'

'What *was* it like?' He eyed her challengingly. 'Do you still think of me as a brother?'

He needed to *ask*? Rose gave him a crooked little smile. 'I just felt as though I'd die if you stopped kissing me.'

His eyes shut in such obvious anguish she put up a hand in alarm.

'Hey—don't worry, James. It was just a few kisses. If that's a problem for you just drive me back and I'll forget they ever happened.'

He raised a dark, disbelieving eyebrow. 'Can you do that?'

'If I have to.'

'Like hell you will!' He yanked her onto his lap and began to kiss her again, pushed her sweater aside to kiss her neck: swift, travelling kisses that set her heart hammering as he slid his hands beneath the heavy white wool to cup her breasts. Rose gasped as he laid them bare and caressed nipples which hardened at their first contact with a man's experienced, coaxing fingers. Streaks of fire shot through her, and she thrust herself against him, locking her hands behind his neck as she gave him back kiss for open-mouthed kiss, until at last it was she who pulled away, and he buried his face in her hair and held her close.

'This is all wrong,' he groaned. 'I shouldn't be doing this.'

Rose stroked his hair. 'It was just a kiss or two, James.'

'But I wanted—still want—a lot more than that.'

'So do I.'

He sat up abruptly, his face stern. 'Don't say things like that, Rose.'

She met his eyes head-on. 'I'm just making it clear I'm as much to blame as you.'

'If I hadn't started it would you have kissed *me*?'

'No way!' Rose smiled crookedly. 'I didn't think you—well—thought of me that way.'

'I didn't think I did, either.' James shook his head slowly. 'It's Greg's fault.'

'Your friend at the track?'

'Yes. When he offered to carry you back this morning I could have thumped him. I almost told him to take his hands off—because you belonged to me.' He smiled a little. 'You can laugh if you like.'

Rose shook her head, a dazed look in her eyes. She slid off his lap and stood up, at a loss how to respond to his mind-blowing revelation. 'It's getting late. I should go.'

James eyed her moodily as he got up. 'You won't be able to run with that foot for a day or two.'

'No.' Rose began tying back her hair to hide her desolation.

'What do you usually do in the evenings?'

'Go for a drink in the union, or see a film. Con's got a VCR so sometimes we rent a video instead.' Rose gave him a wry little smile. 'And sometimes, believe it or not, I just stay in my room and work.'

He smoothed a stray lock of hair back from her forehead, his smile so openly possessive her pulse-rate rocketed. 'So you're not here just to have a good time like some of the others. What do you have in mind to do when you—?'

'Grow up?' said Rose tartly.

'I was going to say qualify, Miss Dryden,' he contradicted, in such ultra refined Morningside accents Rose giggled.

'Miss Jean Brodie to the life.'

'Doubting my sexual preferences again?' he growled, and pulled her into his arms. 'I thought I'd convinced you.'

'Convince me again!' she whispered, and he let out an explosive breath and kissed her so fiercely the difference in their height almost overbalanced them.

'I was wrong,' James groaned at last. 'You're very definitely a girl, complete with a full set of everything to drive a man crazy. And now it *is* time you went.' He thrust her away. 'Go and tidy up in the bathroom. Mrs Bradley will probably want to say goodnight.'

On the short journey back to the flat both of them discussed the film with determination, doing their best to behave as though their passionate exchange had never happened, and when James parked at the entrance to the building Rose said goodnight, shot out of the car and ran up the stairs as fast as her sore foot allowed.

'You're late,' said Con, looking worried.

Fabia pulled Rose into their room, her eyes sparkling. 'How was it? Did he hold your hand in the dark? Did he kiss you goodnight this time?'

'For heaven's sake,' said Rose, laughing. 'I don't ask what you're up to when you're out with Will.'

'Just as well!' Con rolled her eyes, then smiled affectionately. 'You obviously had a great time.'

Rose nodded blissfully. 'We went back to his place. His landlady's nice. She had things ready for us to make sandwiches.'

Fabia pounced. 'Where did you eat them?'

'In his room again.'

'Are we talking bedroom, here?'

'No. It's just a sitting room. He must sleep somewhere else.' Rose yawned. 'Now, if it's all right by you, I'd like to go to bed and get off this foot.'

'Is it still sore?' demanded Con. 'Sit down and show me.'

Rose obediently removed sock and shoe and tore off the dressing, wiggling her foot at the others.

'Seems all right,' said Fabia. 'A bit red and tender-looking, though. I'll slosh on some antiseptic and stick another plaster on for you.'

'You definitely can't go running again for a bit,' said Con regretfully. 'Has Sinclair said anything about another meeting?'

'No.' Rose looked guilty. 'I got out of the car in a rush so he wouldn't think I was hinting at one.'

The phone saved her from a storm of scolding from her friends.

'Yes, she's here,' said Con, eyes sparkling. 'Hang on a second.'

She tossed the receiver to Rose, hauled Fabia bodily out of the room and shut the door.

'Why the blazes did you chase off so fast, Rose?' Demanded James irately. 'You didn't even give me a chance to kiss you goodnight.'

Rose said nothing.

James waited, then sighed in exasperation. 'It's like getting blood out of stone.' He paused. 'I suppose I frightened you silly.'

Was he serious?

'No,' Rose assured him.

'So if I promise to stay at arm's length you'll come out with me again?'

To the ends of the earth, if he liked.

'Yes.'

'Is there someone else in the room?' he demanded.

'No.'

'Then *talk* to me, Rose.'

'What do you want me to say?'

'That you enjoyed our evening as much as I did.'

'You know very well that I did. Every single minute of it,' she added fiercely, in case he was in any doubt.

'That's *better*,' he said with satisfaction. 'So listen. Tomorrow I train with the team, but how about the next night?'

'OK.'

'What would you like to do?'

'Would Mrs Bradley object if I just came round to your place for an hour?' And if he took it for granted she wanted him to make love to her again she didn't care. It was the truth.

'Mrs Bradley thought you were a very charming young lady,' he said, in refined Edinburgh accents again, and Rose giggled. 'I'm in full agreement,' he added, his voice deepening. 'I'll come for you at seven.'

'I'll look forward to it.'

'So will I,' he agreed, with a note in his voice that brought the colour rushing to her cheeks. 'Goodnight, Rose.'

Restless at the memory, Rose got out of bed and went to the kitchen to make more tea. How naive she'd been all those years ago. Young and so trusting she'd been caught in her own snare. With not the slightest hope of success to start with she'd deliberately set out to make James Sinclair fall in love with her, and succeeded beyond her wildest expectations. But in the process she'd fallen helplessly in love in return. Which had been inevitable. If she hadn't had a secret crush on the legendary Sinclair from the start nothing would have induced her to fall in with Con's plan. But that, in common with many other aspects of her love affair, was a secret she'd never shared with anyone. Not even with James.

From the first Rose was obdurate about going out in public with James. Their morning runs and the brief hours spent in his room were the only meetings she would agree to, even repeat trips to the cinema were vetoed in case they were less lucky than the first time, and met someone they knew.

'Why are you so dead set against being seen with me?' he demanded irritably.

'Because you're Sinclair, famous for not socialising with girls. And I'm a lowly first-year. So all your friends—not to mention mine—would be watching every move, tongues hanging out, if they saw us out together.' Rose touched his cheek with a placating hand. 'I just can't bear the idea of everyone speculating about us, spoiling things. Making more of our—our friendship than it is.'

'Friendship,' he growled, and pulled her onto his lap. 'Is this how you behave with all your friends, Miss Dryden?' He kissed her hungrily, his hands busy with her shirt buttons, and Rose moaned as his fingers found her nipples, her response arching her back. James bent his head to take instant advantage, his grazing teeth and clever fingers causing pleasure so intense she could hardly endure it.

Because this was the night Mrs Bradley went to her bridge club they had the house to themselves, a fact Rose was burningly aware of as James made love to her with mounting demand. They had cooked supper together in the kitchen and eaten it there for once, but, sitting knee to knee at the table, the tension between them had increased steadily throughout the meal until by the time they'd reached the privacy of his room they had fallen on each other the moment they were through the door. Kisses and increasingly intimate caresses were the extent of their mutual exploration of each other. So far. But by this time Rose was so madly in love she knew that if James wanted more she would give him everything he wanted. Because she wanted it too. So much it kept her awake at night.

After a while James thrust her from him and retreated to the far corner of the sofa, breathing raggedly. 'This is dangerous,' he said hoarsely.

Rose turned her head away, letting her streaming hair hide her face from him. 'Why?'

'You know very well why.'

'Are you saying I'm a tease?'

'No. But I'm not made of stone. So we can't see each other alone like this any more or the inevitable will happen.' He slanted a half-veiled glance at her. 'I suppose there's no chance of your turning up at the Sceptre on Saturday after the away match?'

Rose shuddered. 'No fear.'

James got up to tower over her, his eyes slitted. 'Why not?'

Rose shook her hair back, turning her face up to him in appeal. 'I keep telling you why not. I'd rather people didn't know we're seeing each other.'

'Is that what we're doing?'

She flushed. 'Sort of.'

'Which just about sums it up.' He glared at her. '*I* would be only too happy to be seen out with you. While you can't stand the thought of it, which does damn all for my self-esteem, lady. I suppose if you lived in actual hall, instead of the flat, I wouldn't even be allowed to pick you up and take you home.'

'No,' she admitted miserably.

'In that case what the hell's the point of it all?' He scowled. 'I refuse to be the skeleton in your cupboard, Rose Dryden. So it's ultimatum time. Come and join me at the Sceptre on Saturday, in front of your friends *and* mine. Or we pack it in—stop seeing each other altogether.'

Rose gazed at him, stricken. Then she got up and took her coat from the back of a chair. 'I just want to stay as we are,' she said miserably, hoping he'd sweep her into his arms and kiss her senseless.

But James did nothing of the kind. His face set in grim lines she'd never seen before, he preceded her down the stairs and took his car keys from the hall table. He opened the front door, and ushered her through it in a hostile silence he kept up all the way back to the flat. When he stopped the car outside her entrance Rose unfastened her seat belt, purposely taking time over it for once to give him a chance to thaw.

'Goodnight, James. Thank you for supper.'

'Goodbye, little girl,' he said coldly, and, far from thawing towards her, drove away the moment Rose closed the passenger door.

Because the flat was empty when she got in, Rose went to bed without interrogation, and cried her eyes out, unheard. Next morning she got up as usual for the early-morning run, but this time James wasn't waiting for her, and it was Greg Prosser, James's rugby-playing team mate, who joined her on the track after she'd completed four endless circuits. Rose gave him a cheery wave and left before she could burst into tears again. When she got back to the flat she took a long shower, then had toast and coffee waiting when her yawning flatmates joined her.

'Right,' said Rose, cutting straight to the chase. 'I think we can all agree that the plan worked?'

'It certainly did—like a charm,' said Con, pushing her hair out of her eyes.

'Mission accomplished, then. But now it's over. If you remember, the idea was to make James Sinclair fall in love with me, not the other way round. So that's it.' Rose smiled brightly. 'Time I got myself back into circulation again.'

Con and Fabia were loud with argument against this, but Rose was adamant. She would not, she declared, be seeing James Sinclair again. And did her utmost to hide her desolation every time the phone rang for one of the other girls. But James, it soon became evident, was not a man to waste time on lost causes. Rose reverted to evenings spent in the union, but by the weekend she was missing James so badly she was willing to agree to anything he wanted, just as long as they could be together again. To demonstrate her change of heart she went to the Sceptre with the others, on fire with barely contained impatience as she waited for the rugby crowd to arrive. But when they did James wasn't with them. Rose's disappointment was so intense she felt physically ill. She forced herself to laugh and flirt as though James's non-appearance was the last thing on her mind, but inside she was hurting badly. And Con, whose eyes saw more than most, tapped Rose on the arm and suggested they left.

'Fabia's coming back with Hargreaves, as usual,' she said. 'So come on. Let's get out of here.'

On the way home Rose confessed that it was Sinclair who'd put a summary end to things between them. 'He wanted us to go out together like a normal couple.'

'And you *refused*?' said Con incredulously. 'Are you out of your mind? Most girls would jump at the chance.'

Rose nodded miserably. 'I know. And I'm sorry now, believe me. But at the time I couldn't bear the thought of everyone watching and making bets on whether we were sleeping together. No one would care a damn if it was some other bloke, of course. But because it's Sinclair it's different.' She swallowed hard. 'I never dreamed he'd stop seeing me altogether, Con. Which serves me right.'

'So ring him.'

Rose's eyes lit with a steely gleam. 'No, I can't do that. Not now.'

'Why not, for heaven's sake?'

'If Sinclair had really wanted to see me he'd have turned up tonight on the off chance I'd be there. He didn't, so that's that. I've got my pride.'

Con smiled in approval. 'Good girl. He's not the only man in the world, Rosie. And it's Valentine's day next week. You'll be knee-deep in partners at the dance.'

To Rose's surprise she received as many cards as Fabia and Con. The flat was awash with red hearts and sentimental verses alongside jokier offerings with messages ranging from the cute to the downright rude. But the card that Rose liked the most was an exquisite watercolour of a single red rose, with no verse at all. And to add to her secret excitement a matching live bloom arrived for her during the morning.

'A rose for Rose,' said the message on the florist's card.

'Dear me, I wonder who that's from?' said Con, smiling.

'No point in wondering,' said Fabia with relish. 'Mystery is the point of it all.'

Rose tried to convince herself that neither card nor rose was from James. Miles Challoner, who fancied himself as a Byronic type, was probably responsible. A thought which dissipated her excitement very thoroughly. In comparison with James Sinclair all other males in her immediate vicinity seemed immature and uninteresting, and with no chance of seeing him there she got ready for the dance later without much enthusiasm. Her dress, bought in Chastlecombe during the January sales, was a little sleeveless number sprigged with rosebuds on black silk, with fluted hem and plunging V-neck, and was pronounced such a success by her friends Rose's spirits lifted a little as Fabia did her make-up. Tonight she would have fun and enjoy herself. And forget James Sinclair.

CHAPTER SIX

To MAKE the evening more of an occasion Con and Fabia had persuaded Rose it would be a good idea to invite a few people round first for a snack supper. By early evening the small flat was a crush of young men in dinner jackets and girls in party frocks. The three hostesses passed round bits and pieces bought from a supermarket to accompany a sparing supply of bubbly wine from the same source, and by the time they got to the dance the entire group was in tearing spirits. While Rose, if not quite as carefree as the others, was feeling a lot better than she'd done for a while, and knew she looked good, for the simple reason that so many of her partners told her so. Miles, as expected, was much in evidence, and extravagant with his praise of her dress.

'Clever girl—roses for Rose,' he whispered in her ear, unaware that he'd damped his partner down so badly she wanted to run from the floor in tears.

Of course James hadn't sent the rose. But like a fool she'd let herself hope he had. Just for a while. She smiled up at Miles with such determined animation he responded with enthusiasm, crushing her so close against him the studs of his dress shirt prodded her painfully through the silk. When the band finished the set Miles put a possessive arm round her to steer her back to the noisy group at their table and Rose slid into a chair next to Con to join in heated, laughing speculation about who had sent Valentine cards to whom. When the college band started up again with a slow number, Will Hargreaves pulled

Fabia to her feet, then stood rooted to the spot, staring at a new arrival near the door. Con muttered incredulously as all eyes turned in the same direction. But Rose couldn't hear a thing over the heartbeat drumming against her ribs at the sight of James Sinclair in formal black and white. With a red rose in his lapel. He began to thread his way through the crowd, causing an audible stir when he came to a halt in front of her.

'Dance with me, Rose?' he said, smiling.

In a flash the evening was transformed. She nodded formally in assent, and went into James's arms like a homing bird, never even noticing the stricken look on Miles Challoner's face.

The knowledge that they were attracting attention on all sides no longer mattered a jot to Rose. Now she was in James Sinclair's arms again the rest of the world could go hang. Unsurprised to find that someone as co-ordinated as James moved well, for a while she just gave herself up to the bliss of the moment, but when they were far enough way from the band to talk she looked up into his intent face.

'You dance well, Sinclair.'

'The academy in charge of my education insisted on such niceties,' he informed her, in mock-refined accents she found so irresistible. Rose gave a bubbling little laugh and he smiled down at her in response as he held her closer, and for a moment they could have been alone in the crowded room. 'Are you having a good time?' he asked politely, his eyes saying something so completely different Rose's breathing quickened.

'The best,' she assured him, which was the simple truth now she was dancing with James Sinclair. 'We had a sort of supper party before the dance to put everyone in the mood.'

'You didn't invite *me*!'

'Of course I didn't.'

'Why not?'

'You know perfectly well why,' she said, her eyes flashing, and he smiled, in the slow, igniting way that took her breath away.

'Do you know how much I've missed you, Rose?'

She gazed up at him steadily. 'Half as much as I've missed you, maybe?'

His eyes blazed as he bent closer. 'Let's go home.'

'Now?'

'Right now. Mrs Bradley's away on holiday, and...' he bent to whisper in her ear '...as you know very well, I make a great bacon sandwich.'

Rose looked up at him for a long considering moment, then noticed a pulse throbbing beside his mouth. So he wasn't sure she'd say yes.

'Ah, well, I never could resist a bacon sandwich,' she said lightly. 'I'll fetch my coat.'

The light in his eyes set Rose on fire. 'I'll be outside. Hurry,' he added urgently.

They were the centre of attention as they parted in the middle of the floor, but Rose didn't even notice. When she emerged with her coat Fabia and Con were waiting for her, looking anxious, their relief touching when Rose told them she was leaving with James.

'Don't wait up,' she said blithely.

'Be careful, love,' said Con, plainly worried by Rose's undisguised radiance.

'Don't be such a killjoy,' admonished Fabia. 'Our little flower has been wilting a bit lately. I prefer her this way. Have fun, Rosebud. See you tomorrow—or whenever.'

James was waiting outside by his car. He settled Rose in the low bucket seat, then got in and leaned over to kiss her fiercely before starting the car. 'Are you angry with me?' he demanded.

'For giving me a kiss?' Rose could afford to be facetious now that all was right with the world again.

'No. For making the next best thing to a public declaration in there just now.' He slanted a triumphant look at her as he drove off. 'I decided it was time to take the war into the enemy's camp.'

'I'm not your enemy, James.'

'You defeated *me*.' He smiled straight ahead. 'I retired to plan new strategy, and decided the best thing was to give you no choice. If I came in black-tie gear to the union—which is not a habit of mine—and asked Miss Rose Dryden to dance, I knew no one would be left in doubt about our relationship.'

'Except me,' said Rose.

'If you wait until we get home I'll explain in full.' He touched a hand fleetingly to hers. 'I've missed you at the track.'

'Not every day, you haven't,' she said tartly. 'I went there the first morning. After our—our disagreement. But you were missing.' She turned accusing eyes on his profile. 'Was that a little dressage, to show me you were calling the shots?'

'Right.'

'It worked.'

'Wrong. I had to fight myself tooth and nail to keep from ringing you afterwards.'

'But you won.'

'On the contrary. I lost.' He shot her a brooding look as they arrived in the familiar house. 'After a couple of days without seeing you I was tempted to ring you and say I'd play it any way you wanted. But, chauvinist that I am, I needed you back on my own terms. My campaign was to be subtle. I'd send you the card and the rose, and then, when you were in a totally weakened state of resistance, I'd invade the dance, complete with rose in my buttonhold like a total idiot, and carry you off the field— what's the matter? Why are you looking at me like that?'

Rose gazed at him with eyes like stars. 'You sent me the card with the rose on it? *And* the rose from the florist?'

He gave her a wry grin. 'Don't tell anyone! My street cred would suffer if it came out that Sinclair sent flowers and Valentine cards.'

'In the plural?'

'Hell, no! Just to you, Rose.' He scowled. 'And just who *did* you think sent them?'

'Miles Challoner.'

'The twit who was all over you tonight?'

'He was certainly *not* all over me,' she retorted hotly.

'It looked like it to me. But why did you think it was him?'

'I suppose he was just referring to my dress. He said something about roses for Rose, like the message on the card, so I crossed you off the list.' She smiled at him demurely. 'He must have sent one of the other cards. Yours was only one of half a dozen I received, Mr Sinclair.'

James leapt out of the car and strode round to pull her from her seat. 'Rattling my cage, Miss Dryden?' He hurried her into the house, then stood looking at her under the hall light. 'Do you want that sandwich?' he whispered.

Rose shook her head impatiently. He drew in a deep breath, removed her coat, then took her hand to pull her upstairs with him, both of them stumbling in sudden haste. When they reached his room James lifted her off her feet against him, backing into the door to close it as he kissed her with an unrestrained longing Rose responded to in kind, her caressing hands as demanding as his.

'Wait!' gasped James, and held her away from him, turning her so that he could slide down the zip of her dress. 'My instinct is to tear it off you,' he said into the back of her neck, 'but it seems a shame when you look so good in it.' He kissed the hollow behind her ear, sending a great shiver through her as he lifted her clear of the dress. Then he stood utterly still, his eyes devouring her as she took the pins from her hair. 'You look even better out of it,' he said hoarsely.

Instead of her usual chain-store underwear Rose was wearing brief scraps of pearl-coloured silk Minerva had given her at Christmas, and felt passionately grateful for her forethought when she saw James couldn't take his eyes off her.

'Are you just going to look at me all night?' she asked unsteadily, shaking her hair back, and he closed the space between them, holding her so close their combined heartbeat thumped in unison.

'Tell me this is what you really want, Rose,' he said, his face oddly stern as his eyes locked with hers.

'I do. More than anything in the world,' she said, with such utter certainty he picked her up, laid her on the bed and stripped off the shirt she'd been trying to pull off him with such haste a moment before.

Rose smiled with sudden delight as she realised where she was. 'This is your sofa, James!'

'By day,' he agreed, responding with the slow smile she'd missed so badly. 'At night it's a bed. My bed. And,' he added softly, letting himself down beside her, 'you're the first to share it with me.'

Rose gave a deep, relishing sigh as his arms locked around her. Then she remembered something his ought to know. 'James,' she whispered, then buried her face against his chest.

He tensed. 'What is it, sweetheart? Second thoughts?'

'No!' Rose drew away and met his eyes, her face hot. 'But now seems a good time to mention that Minerva sent me off for contraceptive pills last summer, before I came here.'

His eyes lit with laughter. 'How very practical. Your aunt was obviously a student herself, once.'

Rose nodded, rubbing her flushed cheek against his. 'She warned me that the main student pastimes are drinking and sleeping, quite a lot of the last bit with each other.'

'I'd like to meet this aunt of yours!' James looked amused. 'Though wasn't she worried you'd rush off to put the pills to the test?'

'No. Minerva made it plain she expected me to be— well, discriminate.'

'And you have been?' he said softly.

'Up to now, yes,' said Rose candidly, and smiled into his eyes as she wriggled closer. 'I've certainly never slept with a man before.'

'Did I mention sleeping?'

'No. Which is just as well—I'm not the least bit tired.'

James gave a smothered, delighted laugh, and kissed her, and Rose locked her hands behind his head, surrendering her mouth and body to him with trusting lack of restraint as he removed the last of their clothes. But when they held each other close in full, naked contact, for the first time at last, Rose was startled to find that James was shaking almost as much as she was.

'I haven't done this before myself, but I was rather hoping *you* had,' she said in dismay.

'Of course I have.' He kissed the hollow between her

breasts. 'But never with someone new to it all. At this moment I want you more than I've ever wanted anything in my entire life, but I can't make it perfect for you because I'll have to hurt you.'

'It can't hurt that much,' she said, with a confidence which proved misplaced, because though James kissed and caressed her at such length she thought she'd die if he didn't take her at last, Rose couldn't control an involuntary gasp of anguish when he did.

'Sweetheart,' he groaned, and lay very still, giving Rose time to adjust to the overwhelming intimacy of physical possession.

'I want you to move,' she said gruffly after a moment or two, and James obliged, with a lack of haste which took superhuman effort, Rose could tell, as her hands smoothed the knotted tension of his shoulders. But when she began to experience delicious ripples of sensation in response to the rhythm of his loving James kissed her fiercely, moving with new, demanded urgency, and Rose thrust her hips against him in instinctive, wanton response. But all too soon he groaned like a man in pain as the inexorable delight defeated him, and he buried his face in her neck and gasped in the throes of release as she held him tightly, glorying in the fact that he was suddenly so helpless in her arms.

At last James raised his head and looked deep into her eyes. 'I'm so *sorry*, sweetheart. I wanted it to be so good for you—'

'Oh, but it was,' she assured him, with such fervour she felt him relax against her.

'Next time,' he assured her, 'it will be as wonderful for you as it was for me, I promise.'

And, sooner than Rose had thought humanly possible, even for a superbly fir specimen like James Sinclair, he began to make love to her again. And this time the heat built up slowly, mounting inside her until every inch of her responsive, throbbing body took fire as he coaxed her to heights of physical pleasure which left her lying limp in his arms afterwards, sated from her first experience of sexual fulfilment.

'You were right,' she breathed against his chest. 'It *was* wonderful. Out of this world.' She took a deep, relishing breath. 'I had no idea it would be like that.'

'Neither had I.' James drew the covers over them and held her close, but Rose drew away to look at him.

'You must have known!'

He shook his head, his eyes so gloatingly possessive she shivered with delight. 'This was different. Just knowing that everything we did was the first time for you rocketed me to such an incredible state of arousal it was all new to me, too. But second time round I managed to stay in control. For a while, at least.' He smoothed the tumbled hair from her face, and sighed heavily. 'Rose, it's very late. I don't want to let your go, but it's time I drove you back.'

'I suppose so,' she said without enthusiasm, and wriggled closer.

'If you do that,' he said breathlessly, 'I'll never let you go.'

On the way back to campus later James sprang a surprise. 'Mrs Bradley's away at her daughter's place for a week. Come and stay with me until she comes back.'

'Won't she mind when she finds out?' said Rose, utterly ravished by the idea.

'I don't know. I've never had anyone to stay before. But I'm sure she won't.' James slanted a grin at her. 'As I told you before, she thinks it's high time I had a "nice young lady" like you.'

If only the young lady were as nice as he believed, thought Rose guiltily, fighting off a sudden need to confess.

'Well? Will you come?' he repeated.

She eyed him doubtfully. 'Won't I interfere with your work?'

'Bring some of your own. And if we don't get much work done a little break won't do either of us any harm. In fact,' he added, as he drew up outside her building, 'the kind of break I've got in mind will do me a hell of a lot of good. Will you come?'

'Try to keep me away!' said Rose recklessly, and kissed him with a fervour which met with such approval it was a long time before James let her go.

'I'll be round for you in the morning,' he said huskily. 'About ten. Be ready.'

When Rose crept into the flat it was in darkness. She collected pyjamas and dressing gown, then lay in a hot bath, her eyes dreamy as she relieved the incredible events of the night. So that was what it was all about. Viewing it from a theoretical point of view in the past, Rose had always found it difficult to understand why the act of love was something people wanted to do so much. Now she knew exactly why. And pitied females who'd learned about it from lesser men than James. How lucky she was. Though she didn't deserve to be. She'd deliberately set out to make James want her. And, miraculously, he did. Enough to come to the dance tonight and demonstrate it so plainly that now everyone on campus knew that Rose Dryden had somehow managed to bag Sinclair, the man with no time for women.

Rose sat up at last and began to soap herself, her face hot as she found her skin marked with fingerprints in places, which clenched inner muscles at the memory of how she'd acquired them. She dried herself quickly, pulling on pyjamas in a sudden hurry to get to bed and go through every detail of the enchanted night again.

But when she opened the bathroom door Rose found Con waiting for her, looking anxious.

'Come into our room for a bit, Rose. Fabia's making hot chocolate. Once we heard you come in we just had to know you were all right before we could get some sleep.'

'Everything's fine. Wonderful, in fact,' said Rose, her eyes shining.

'Yes.' Con sighed heavily. I can see that. I just wish I hadn't been responsible for it all. I feel like Dr Frankenstein.'

Rose shook her head. 'It isn't your fault. You didn't force me to carry out your plan. And no offence, Con, but it's James who's responsible for my present state of euphoria.'

'I know!'

'Everyone at the dance knows now,' said Fabia, coming in with a tray. 'Miles looked ready to slit his wrists when you left.' She sighed gustily. 'It was so romantic. Just like Richard Gere and Julia Roberts in *An Officer and a Gentleman*—only Sinclair didn't actually carry you out.'

'And it was Debra Winger not Julia Roberts,' said Con dryly, handing a steaming beaker to Rose.

'Whoever. The effect was the same.' Fabia patted the bed beside her. 'Come and sit down, Rosie. I take it that you and Sinclair are now officially a couple?'

'I suppose so.' Rose took refuge in her drink. 'Actually,' she said into the mug, 'I'm going to stay with him at his place for a few days. His landlady's away.'

Con stared at her aghast. 'For pity's sake, Rose, isn't that going a bit far?' She thrust her hands through her pale hair. 'Damn. I feel so *responsible*. I wish I'd never mentioned that wretched plan.'

'I'm very glad you did,' said Rose dreamily. 'Otherwise—'

'Otherwise you'd never have come into contact with Sinclair, and I'm beginning to think that might be a jolly good thing!'

'Why, Con?' demanded Fabia. 'Rose had to—er—cut her teeth on someone, some time. So why not Sinclair?'

'Because,' said Con patiently, 'he'll be leaving in the summer, and Rose won't.'

'I'll meet that problem when I come to it,' promised Rose. 'And don't worry, Con. It's no big deal—just a college romance like everyone else's.'

'Not quite! If it hadn't been for that hare-brained plan of mine it would never have happened.'

Rose gave her a reassuring smile. 'Nothing would have made me go along with it if I hadn't wanted to.' She raised her right hand. 'And I solemnly swear I won't drown you both in tears when it's over.'

The following morning Rose told James to come up when he rang the bell, and not only introduced him formally to Con and Fabia, but made coffee for everyone. The four of them spent a lively half-hour together before Rose handed over her bag to James and said she was ready to leave.

'So,' said James, in the car, 'I take it my relationship with Miss Rose Dryden is now well and truly out in the open?'

'Yes,' said Rose serenely. 'At least, I told Con and Fabia to give truthful answers if—when—questions are asked.'

'And what will they say? That I'm your lover?'

Rose shot him an outraged glance. 'No way! They were instructed to say we're just good friends.'

'Which means everyone will definitely think we're lovers,' he said with satisfaction.

'The circles I move in refer to it as "going out together",' said Rose primly.

James gave her a leer. 'Whereas in actual fact we're going to stay in together.'

'All the time?'

He stopped the car in Henley Crescent and reached in the back for her bag. 'We can go to the cinema, if you like, or out for a meal. Never let it be said I'm a skinflint. But it's my turn, now, to draw the line at any venue where we're likely to run into mutual friends. And *not*, like you, because I don't want to be seen in public with you. I don't care a damn about the things that cause *you* such hangups. But right now we've got the chance of a whole week together, Rose, and I'm damned if I'm going to waste a second of it with other people.'

'Did you mind staying for coffee at the flat, then?' she asked as they went indoors.

James dumped down her bag and took her into his arms. 'No, because I knew you were showing me that you've finished with all that hole-and-corner stuff you were into before.' He kissed her nose. 'When Mrs Bradley's back you can invite your friends round here, if you like.'

Rose leaned back against his linked hands. 'No. I'd rather not. This is our special, private place. Come to the flat instead, If you'd like to.'

'Of course I'd like to.' James pulled her close. 'I didn't sleep much last night,' he said into her hair.

'Neither did I.' She let out a deep, euphoric sigh. 'I was happy just to stay awake and dream.'

For the first time since either of them had started at university neither James Sinclair nor Rose Dryden did a stroke of actual work for an entire week. Instead they cooked meals together, talking on every subject under the sun, and if the weather was fine they drove out of town to find a place to walk, or if it was wet stayed indoors and listened to music or watched television. On two of the evenings James went off to train with the rugby team, but otherwise they were never apart for more than a minute. And, as though it was something too precious to squander, they made love only at night when James converted his sofa into a bed.

Rose soon learned that her first experience of sexual love had been a mere foretaste of the delight possible when two people came together intent on giving each other pleasure.

'Though pleasure seems a milk-and-water kind of word to describe what happens between us,' said Rose one night, and turned her head to meet the half-veiled eyes intent on her face.

'You're the English student. What word would you choose?' asked James, smoothing a hand down her spine.

'You'll laugh.'

'No I won't.'

She kept her eyes on his. 'For me what happened just now was sheer rapture. And if that sounds too mushy and over the top, you did ask.'

'It sounds exactly right,' he said huskily. 'And I have a theory as to why.'

'Yes?'

'Is there a possibility that what we feel for each other is something a tad more cerebral than lust?' he said gravely.

Rose bit her lip, afraid to commit herself.

'Cat got your tongue?' he asked affably. 'Don't be frightened, Rose. I was merely pointing out that maybe we're attracted to each other for more than just our bodies. Or am I imagining the rapport we enjoy out of bed as well as in it?'

'No.'

James shook his head, resigned. 'Just no?'

'Yes. I mean you're not imagining it.'

'Good.' He trailed a finger down her cheek. 'You do realise that we've spent five days—and nights—in each other's company, now, and except for a heated argument or two on world issues we've lived together in remarkable harmony?'

As if she needed reminding!

'I'm very easy to get on with,' said Rose demurely.

'While I'm anything but, as a rule.'

'I think you are,' she said fiercely, and kissed him.

'Thank you.' He held her closer. 'But if you talked with some of the people I roomed with when I first came here they'd disagree, I promise you. I shared a student flat something like yours, only with three other guys. They were younger than me, straight out of school, first time away from home, and hell-bent on drinking and womanising. While my sole interests were study and sport. It made for a bad situation all round.'

'So what happened?'

'I looked around for lodgings and found this place before my second term. Mrs Bradley was newly widowed, and had decided to let a couple of rooms to students.' He paused. 'I persuaded her to make it one student only. Unlike most students, I had some money of my own.'

'From your father?'

'No. He left everything to my mother. But when she sold the family home Mother made the proceeds over to me, and Donald put me on to a financial adviser who helped me invest it in a way which gives me an income. Not vast, but enough to compensate Mrs Bradley for taking me on as her sole lodger.'

Rose was impressed. 'Most boys of eighteen with cash would have gone on a spending spree.'

James grinned. 'I was normal enough to splurge on the car when I got back from Oz.'

'That's a relief—nice to know you're human.' She rubbed her cheek against his thoughtfully. 'So you're the only lodger Mrs Bradley's ever had, then?'

'Right.' He turned her face up to his. 'Though I prefer to think of myself as the only lover Rose Dryden's ever had.'

She gazed back at him speculatively. 'You like to be first, or the best, at everything, don't you?'

'I suppose you're right,' he agreed, after thought.

Rose eyes him militantly. 'Is that why you made love to me? Because you knew you'd be the first?'

'Hell no! It was part of it,' he added honestly. 'But the main reason was my gut feeling that you and I belonged together. I just couldn't handle the thought of you with someone else.'

'You wouldn't have had to,' she assured him. 'After meeting you I couldn't handle that, either.'

'Then you feel the same?'

Rose nodded. 'Haven't I demonstrated that with unmaidenly lack of inhibition?'

'Yes. But you haven't said so in as many words.'

'What do you want me to say?'

James pushed her flat and knelt over her, a lock of dark hair falling over his forehead as he captured her hands to spread them wide. 'Tell me exactly how you feel about me,' he demanded.

Rose felt like a moth pinned to a board by the relentless, glittering eyes. 'This isn't fair,' she protested.

'All's fair in love and war,' he assured her, and let himself down on top of her, taking her breath away. 'And this, my darling Rose, is love. On my part, anyway.' He kissed her hungrily, his fingers moving over her in sweeping arpeggios of such exquisite sensation she yielded herself up to him helplessly. Then his mouth followed his fingers to shock her with a caress so new and intimate she gasped and writhed, until at last he surrendered to her frantic pleas and surged between her parted thighs to take them rapidly towards climax.

But at the very brink James held her there, his body suddenly still.

'Say it,' he commanded hoarsely, and Rose, totally beyond coherent thought, obeyed.

'I *love* you,' she gasped, raking her nails down his back, and with a growl of triumph James kissed her fiercely and brought them both to glory.

CHAPTER SEVEN

ROSE woke with tears on her face, aching with the familiar feeling of loss and regret ten years had never managed to dispel. And realised she was propped upright against the pillows with all the lights on. When she remembered exactly why, she noticed the time, and shot out of bed, cursing the anonymous pest as she rushed at top speed instead of making her usual gradual transition into the working day.

'Gosh, you look a bit frazzled,' said Bel, when Rose let her in. 'Good thing I start work early on Saturdays. Here, take the post and shut yourself in the office with some coffee. Late night?' she added archly.

'No. Usual time. I just couldn't get to sleep.' Rose pulled a face. 'But if I look that bad I'll take advantage of your offer. Wouldn't do to frighten off the customers.' She hesitated. 'Look, this is for your ears only, Bel. I've had a couple of anonymous phonecalls.'

Bel grinned. 'Querying your taste in underwear?'

'No. Just a bit of heavy breathing, then he whispers my name and rings off. And, before you ask, the number was withheld.' Rose pulled a face. 'It seems silly now, in broad daylight, but it wasn't at all funny late last night.'

'I should say not! That's *nasty*, Rose. Any idea who it could be?'

'No. But coming on top of the Valentine card and the rose, I don't like it one bit.'

Bel eyed her warily. 'I asked Mark if he'd sent the card, by the way.'

'You did *what*?'

'It wouldn't be the first time.'

'We were just kids then,' Rose protested.

'A fact my brother pointed out. He promises to remember next year.' Bel looked worried. 'But where the heavy breather's concerned unplug the phone tonight and use your mobile instead. What did Anthony say about it?'

'Haven't told him.'

Bel looked disapproving. 'I suppose he denied sending the card and the rose?'

'Emphatically.' Rose smiled wryly. 'In fact he was quite hacked off about the whole thing.'

'I bet he was.' Bel swallowed her coffee and patted Rose on the shoulder. 'I'll hold the fort out there. You stay in here and recover.'

By the end of the day Rose was so tired she couldn't bring herself to cope with the paperwork left from the night before. Sunday morning without fail, she promised it, and went upstairs to fall apart for a while before she even thought of making herself some supper. When the phone rang her heart skipped a beat—until she heard Anthony's voice on the message.

'How are you, Rose?' he asked when she picked up.

'Tired. But otherwise, fine. Busy day today.'

'Rose, have you thought any more about contacting your husband?'

Oh, yes. She'd thought of it. 'I'll get round to it eventually.'

'Remember that you're not obliged to *speak* to him, Rose. After all these years you can just inform him of your intention. Or have a solicitor do it for you.'

'I know all that, Anthony.'

'Do it, then,' he urged. 'I'll call you on Monday.'

Much as Rose rather objected to his peremptory attitude, she knew Anthony was right. It was high time she set herself free. But not to get married again. Once was enough.

She'd known where James Sinclair worked ever since his promotion before the age of thirty to executive vice-presidency of a prestigious merchant bank. Fabia Hargreaves had sent her an article about him she'd cut out from the financial section of one of the Sunday papers. And had unsettled Rose for days afterwards. She knew perfectly well she should to have done something about divorce years before. But the article had revived her stubborn determination to make James the first to act.

While Rose ate her supper she came to a decision. She would write to James at the bank. Then the ball would be in his court. And if he chose not to reply, she would just carry on with the divorce now she knew the court would grant this whether James agreed or not. Not that he had any reason to refuse. He must surely be as eager to be free as she was by this time.

Rose got out her laptop and composed a brief, purposely formal letter, informing James Sinclair of her intention. Then, before she could change her mind, went out in the early evening quiet to post it. After the shops closed Chastlecombe always enjoyed a lull before it came to life again for Saturday night, and the only person Rose met was Elise Fox, who sold expensive clothes and jewellery at the other end of the cobbled arcade. After they'd chatted together for a few minutes Rose went back home, unlocked her private door, then stopped dead in her tracks. A fresh red rose lay on the floor. And it very definitely hadn't been there when she'd left. Rose snatched up the flower with a shaking hand, her heart thumping as she looked up the stairs. Could someone have got in while she was out? No. Of course not. Her tormentor must have pushed the rose through the letter box while she was talking to Elise.

Suddenly Rose lost her temper. The man might be intent on frightening her, but no way was she going to let him succeed. She slammed the door shut, stormed up the stairs and hurled the flower in the bin to join the other one. Then she unplugged the phone and turned her radio on at almost full volume while she made herself supper. And later that night, when Rose went to bed, she pushed the extra pillows away and switched off the light, determined to sleep.

Sunday lunch with Minerva and her husband, Henry Beresford, was congenial as usual, and afterwards Minerva sent her husband off for a nap so she could catch up on shop talk with her niece. But instead of giving her aunt an update on business at the shop, after a few stops and starts Rose finally came out with her long overdue confession.

Minerva, elegant in tailored trousers and dark blue rollneck sweater, showing only a few threads of silver in her black Dryden hair, heard Rose out in astonished silence. 'My poor child!' she said at last, giving Rose a compassionate hug. 'I knew there was something desperately wrong that summer, of course. But when you came back from Portugal you looked so much better I assumed you'd recovered from what I took to be a college romance gone wrong.' Cobalt-blue eyes twinkled at Rose. 'I'd had a few myself, remember. Though marriage was the last thing on the agenda with any of the wretches lusting after *me*. Anyway, don't worry about it any more, pet. Henry will see to everything for you the minute you give him the go ahead.'

Feeling as if a burden had been lifted, Rose decided to

wait for a few days to give James Sinclair time to reply
to her letter. If he didn't, the following Monday she would
instruct Henry to start divorce proceedings anyway.
Decision made, she felt better. There were no more menacing phone calls, no more roses pushed through her letter
box. Life, decided Rose, had returned to normal. On the
Thursday evening she dealt with paperwork for an hour
after shutting up shop, ate a substantial meal for once, and
was just clearing away after supper when the bell rang
below on her private door.

Rose hesitated. At one time she would have run down
to open it without a second thought. Instead she went into
her bathroom, the only place with the necessary view. But
under one of the artistic street lights in the cobbled court-
yard the only thing visible was the top of an unknown
male head, and a second ring of the doorbell sent her
hurrying downstairs to open the door as far as the safety
chain allowed.

'Yes?' she said, with a polite smile, her eyes widening
in sudden shock when her visitor turned to face her. White
streaks in thick black hair gave a fleeting impression of
age quickly cancelled by a lean, instantly familiar face.
And from the hot surge of excitement thrusting up inside
her Rose realised that this was exactly what she'd hoped
for when she'd written the letter. She stared at her visitor
in wordless recognition, while ten years vanished in the
wink of an eye. Then excitement gave way to remembered
pain and humiliation, and her eyes narrowed in hostility
as they met her visitor's assessing gaze.

'Hello, Rose,' said James Sinclair at last. 'I was in the
area so I thought I'd take a chance on finding you in.'

At the sound of his voice Rose recovered her own.
'James Sinclair, no less.' She gave a swift look round the

arcade, and unhooked the chain. 'I suppose you'd better come inside,' she said coolly.

'Thank you.' He waited in the small entry until she'd locked and bolted the door, then followed as she led the way up to the sitting room.

'Can I get you a drink?' she asked, caught so much off guard she cursed James Sinclair for surprising her at the end of a working day. After all these years, it would have been good to have brushed her hair, at least, before coming face to face with him again.

'Thank you. I'm not driving, so a finger of Scotch would be good if you have it.'

Not driving. Was he staying at the King's Head, then? Rose poured whisky into a tumbler, strangling a hysterical laugh at the idea of James Sinclair in the same hotel bed Anthony Garrett used.

She handed over the glass, sat down in her usual chair and waved James to the sofa. 'Do sit down,' she said, icily polite.

'May I take off my jacket?' he asked, equally courteous.

'Of course.'

James unzipped a suede windbreaker, laid it aside and sat down, looking so much at ease Rose felt fiercely resentful. Instead of the city suit expected of the well-dressed banker, he wore a heavy fawn sweater with khaki canvas jeans, and looked altogether far more comfortable and relaxed than she felt he had any right to. But even at twenty-two James had always been self-contained. Except in bed.

'You wear your hair shorter now,' he commented, surprising her.

Rose thrust it behind her ears impatiently. 'So what

brings you here, James? I never imagined you'd come in
person when I wrote the letter.'

'Why not?'

'Lack of time—and interest, maybe?'

'I was due a break. And I own to a great *deal* of interest
about your reasons for waiting so long to divorce me.' He
finished the contents of his glass, looking at her over the
rim. 'You could have done that any time this past five
years with no problem. Why didn't you?'

Rose shrugged indifferently. 'A very childish reason,
I'm afraid. I always promised myself you'd have to ask
first. I never bothered to research the subject, so I've only
just found out you had no need to ask by this time.'

James smiled. And she wished he hadn't. The smile
was familiar. So, to her dismay, was its effect on her.

'For my own part I've never had the slightest desire for
a divorce,' he informed her.

Rose raised a scornful eyebrow. 'You surprise me. At
one stage weren't you worried I might start proceedings
and demand half your worldly goods?'

'By the time I had any worldly goods to speak of too
much time had elapsed for you to do that. Actually,' he
added blandly, 'I've always found it rather an advantage
to be married.'

'Saves trouble where women are concerned, I suppose.'

'Exactly.' He gazed at her in silence for a while, until
Rose began to feel restive under the bright, searching
scrutiny. 'So tell me. Why *do* you want a divorce, Rose?'

'For the obvious reason. I'm thinking of getting married. Again, I mean.' Which was an outright lie. Anthony
was the only one thinking of marriage.

'Just thinking?' He raised an eyebrow. 'Does this mean
you're already co-habiting with someone?'

'No,' she said evenly. 'I've tried that in the past. It was a mistake.'

His face hardened. 'Unflattering.'

'I wasn't referring to *you*, James.' She smiled coldly. 'Other men have featured in my life over the past ten years.'

His eyes roved over her impersonally. 'Which have been kinder to you than to me, Rose.'

'Your hair surprised me,' she admitted. 'How long has it been like that?'

'I wish I could be melodramatic and say the white streaks arrived overnight after you left me,' he said sardonically, 'but they started creeping in about five years ago. Not that I mind,' he added. 'They lend suitable gravitas to someone bent on a fast-track career in banking.'

'You're determined to be the youngest chief executive ever, I suppose?'

'Something like that.' James eyed her assessingly. 'How did you know where to contact me?'

'Fabia Hargreaves—she was Dennison when I shared a flat with her—sent me a cutting about your promotion. So I just had to check you were still with the same bank before I wrote.'

'I see.' He looked round at the room. 'You live here alone?'

'Yes.'

'What happened to your aunt?'

'Minerva surprised everyone by getting married last year. When she asked me if I fancied managing the shop for her I jumped at it. She still owns it, but to all intents and purposes it's mine to run as I like.'

He sat looking at her in silence for a while. 'And is life in a small country town like this satisfying for you?'

'Yes. I'd had enough city lights by the time I came

back here. I'd lived in London ever since I left college. Which,' Rose added, 'is more than enough about me. So tell me, James, are you getting married, too?'

'No. I was tricked into marriage once.' The grey eyes were steely. 'I rarely make the same mistake twice.'

'I didn't trick you,' she said wearily.

'That's a lie, Miss Dryden.' His mouth tightened. 'I doubt you've ever called yourself Mrs Sinclair.'

'Absolutely not.'

There was silence in the room for a while, until at last Rose couldn't help repeating her question. 'What's your real reason for coming here, James? We could have settled all this by letter.'

He looked at her levelly. 'When I saw your signature on that terse little missive it reminded me of unfinished business between us.'

Suddenly the air crackled between them, all pretence of civility vanished.

'It all seemed very final to me!' Her eyes flashed malevolently. 'You told me to get out of your life, so I did. What's unfinished about that?'

'I wasn't thinking straight at the time,' he rapped. 'I was only twenty-two, for God's sake—'

'And I was only eighteen,' she cut back. 'No match for you at all. I would never have dreamed you could be so vicious.'

His mouth tightened. 'I was hurt, and angry, and so bloody disillusioned I hit out in the worst way I could think of.'

'The very worst,' she agreed stonily. 'Your timing was diabolical. In the middle of my first-year exams. You'd done yours, of course. Belated congratulations, by the way. I heard you got your double first.'

'And despite everything you passed *your* exams, too.'

'Just. Which was something of a miracle under the circumstances. And such a struggle I didn't do as well as forecast. I took off abroad for the entire summer to try and get over you.' Her lip curled. 'Looking back, it seems such utter nonsense now. That I could have let a man affect me so badly, I mean. But at the time all I wanted was to forget I'd ever met you, let alone married you.'

'Did you succeed?'

'Oh, yes.' Rose gave him a frosty smile. 'Hearts mend. Though nothing would have convinced me of that at the time.'

'So where did you go? When I couldn't find you I contacted your aunt, but she just said you were working abroad.'

'Minerva knew someone who needed a nanny for the summer in Portugal. The family offered me the job, and, painful as it was in one way, I jumped at it, desperate to get away.'

James Sinclair's hard eyes narrowed. 'Why was it painful?'

Rose controlled herself with effort. 'Sensitive soul, aren't you? I had honestly believed I was expecting a baby shortly before, if you remember. When I found I wasn't I was utterly shattered. And bitterly disappointed. Unlike you,' she added bitterly. 'You said some foul, unforgivable things last time we met.'

His face set. 'Would it make you feel better if I told you I regretted them later?'

'Please don't bother. It's a very long time since any of that mattered in the slightest to me.' Rose got up, sure he'd take the hint and go if she offered him another drink. 'Can I give you a refill?'

'Thank you.' James surrendered his glass, ignoring the icy look she gave him as she took it. 'Rose,' he said slowly, when she'd given him a meagre half-inch of single malt, 'hearing from you out of the blue reminded me of some loose ends I'd never tied up. I won't pretend I've been thinking of you *all* the time over the years, but from time to time I'd remember, and wonder.'

'About what, in particular?'

'Don't pretend you don't know!' His eyes speared hers. 'Tell me the truth at last, Rose. Did you really set out to trap me?'

'Oh, all that nonsense.' Rose shrugged airily. 'I certainly tried hard to make you fall in love with me, but there was no trap involved. The master plan was Cornelia Longford's brainchild, in actual fact, but I plead guilty to carrying it out.'

The cold eyes narrowed dangerously. 'So you really did follow a plan!'

'To the letter. Con worked out a sort of blueprint. Phase one, phase two, and so on. It all worked like the proverbial charm, too.' She felt a surge of primitive satisfaction at the look on his face.

'You deliberately baited your hook, and I swallowed it, line and sinker,' he said in disgust.

Secretly revelling in the effect her information had on her listener, Rose described the way her friends had gleaned information about the legendary Sinclair's background and tastes so she could pretend common interests. 'I must have been mad,' she added wryly. 'Up to then my sole effort at keeping fit was an occasional aerobics session. But Con insisted I went to the track to run into you accidentally.'

'You actually took up running that early in the morning just to bump into me?' he said blankly.

'I blush to think of it now,' she admitted. 'Up to that time I'd only run for a bus. I pretended to like foreign films, too, which I didn't all that much, and holidays on Skye, though I'd never actually been there. But perhaps you've forgotten all that.'

'I remember every last thing,' he said grimly. 'My God, I've often thought since that I'd been too ready to condemn. But that poisonous little tick was right after all. You were guilty as charged.'

'Who do you mean?' she said swiftly.

'Fair-haired twit, always mooning after you.'

'So Miles was the culprit,' said Rose with relief. 'I'm so glad.'

'*Glad!*'

'At the time I suspected Fabia, even Con, because they were the only ones in the know.'

'Your precious Miles managed to find out, too. He took great pleasure in cornering me to tell me about your plan,' said James grimly. 'I didn't believe him at first, told him to get lost before I rearranged his face—'

'But when you confronted me with it I confessed, of course, and topped it by giving you the glad news that you needn't have married me after all,' said Rose with a brittle smile.

James finished the drink and stood up. 'Oddly enough,' he said, his eyes wintry, 'I didn't regret marrying you, Rose. I was crazy about you. But at that point I was so dog-tired from working my brains out I just couldn't handle it when you hit me with the news about the false alarm only minutes after Miles had told me about your famous plan. It was a double body blow to every illusion I had. Which is why I went berserk.'

Rose went to the door. 'Look, James, I confess I did set out to make you fall in love with me. Though, heaven knows, it just seems like a silly student prank now.' She turned to face him, her eyes as cold as his. 'But think for a minute. No one can really make another human being fall in love. Not that you did that, of course. If you had you'd have listened to me, trusted me, and found out what really happened.'

His eyes narrowed. 'I'm listening now. I've come a long way to listen. So go on. Tell me your side of it.'

'You know it already,' she said impatiently. 'I was late one month. I panicked.'

'But you were taking contraceptive pills. Or told me you were.'

'I was. Religiously. But, if you remember, I had a stomach bug which laid me low for a few days. I knew that could stop the pills from doing their job. So when—when my period was late, which had never happened before, I was in such a state I was convinced I was pregnant.'

'But I thought the tests were pretty accurate.'

Rose flushed hectically, and looked away. 'It sounds brainless now, but it never occurred to me to get one. I was even throwing up by that stage—sheer nerves, as it turned out—so I was convinced. By the time I told you I was in a terrible state.'

'And I was such a stiff-necked, high-minded idiot,' said James without emotion, 'that I did the time-honoured thing and married you the first moment I could. I was so shell-shocked I never even asked if you'd had a test.'

Silence fell between them, lengthening until Rose's nerves were stretched to breaking point by the time James spoke again.

'One thing I'm still in the dark about, Rose. When you were concocting this famous plan, why the hell did you choose me?'

'Oh I didn't *choose* you.' She gave him a patronising little smile. 'In the beginning all three of us were going to try the plan out with different men, so we wrote names on bits of paper. I drew yours out of the hat.'

'Good God!' His brows drew together incredulously. 'You mean that everything that happened was just by chance?'

'Afraid so.' There was little point, now, in admitting that she'd had an outsize crush on him long before Con's famous plan. He was no more likely to believe her now than he would have back then, on the never-to-be-forgotten day when he'd heard his quixotic chivalry had been unnecessary after all.

'Amazing,' said James, shrugging into his jacket. 'Two lives changed out of all recognition by the luck of the draw.'

'Fate has a strange sense of humour,' agreed Rose coolly.

James looked at her for a long, contemplative moment. 'I'm glad I made the effort to come and see you. You've grown into your bones, Rose. You look good.'

'So do you,' she said, magnanimous now he was leaving. 'I rather like the hair.'

'Thank you.' He gave her the slow, inflammatory smile she'd never quite managed to forget. 'How very civilised we are!'

'That was my aim when I wrote to you,' she pointed out. 'To go about things in a civilised way, instead of informing you through a solicitor.'

When the phone interrupted them Rose excused herself to pick it up, then breathed in sharply as the caller whispered her name and rang off.

'What's the matter?' asked James, as she crashed the receiver back. He grabbed her by the wrists. 'Rose, for God's sake what's wrong? You're as white as a sheet!'

She gave him a shaky smile. 'Nuisance phone call.'

James released her to stab in the recall numbers, but again the number had been withheld. 'Has this happened before?' he demanded.

'Yes. This is the third. But there are the roses, too.'

'What roses?'

Seized by a sudden need to unburden herself, Rose explained, then gave James a wry little smile. 'At least I know it's not you.'

'Me?' His eyes narrowed ominously. 'You actually believed I'd deliberately frighten you like this?'

She shrugged. 'After a silence of ten years it seems a silly idea now, but I couldn't help wondering for a moment or two. By coincidence the card was very much like the one you sent me once. But the choice of a rose is pretty obvious for someone who knows my name.'

He eyed her warily. 'Your new man couldn't be the culprit?'

'Certainly not,' she snapped. 'Anthony was very annoyed by the card. And the first of the roses. But I haven't told him about the calls, or the second flower.'

'I think you'd better. What does the caller say?'

'Just breathes a bit and whispers my name.' She shivered. 'I sat up all night with the lights on when he rang after midnight the other night.'

'Tell the police,' James ordered brusquely. 'It may be just a rose and a phone call at this stage, but stalking can lead to something a hell of a sight more serious.'

'You think it's a stalker?' she said, horrified.

'It could be.' James looked at her with open concern. 'Rose, I don't like the thought of leaving you alone after this. Isn't there someone who could come to stay with you tonight?'

'Of course there is. Or I could go to Minerva if I wanted

to. But I don't.' Her jaw tightened. 'I flatly refuse to let this joker affect my life.'

He smiled wryly. 'You were always a feisty little thing.'

'Obstinate's the word,' she said, pulling a face, then shivered a little. 'But I admit to being a bit spooked by this.'

James looked grim. 'So tell the police. In the meantime, I'll stay for a while. At least until your colour comes back.'

'Thank you. I could do with some company. Even—' Rose halted, flushing at the gleam in the grey eyes.

'Even mine, Rose?'

'I don't mean to be rude,' she said stiffly. 'I've tried not to let this business get to me, but it's difficult. I thought it was amusing in the beginning, but it isn't any more. I really loathe the feeling that somebody's out there, watching me.'

'If he's watching you tonight at least he'll know you're not alone. And if the phone rings,' he added with menace, 'I'll answer it, and make sure your caller thinks twice about ringing you again.'

CHAPTER EIGHT

OF ALL the things she'd intended to do that evening, drinking coffee with James Sinclair was the last Rose had pictured when she'd shut up shop for the night. Taking time out for repairs to her face and hair, she went back to the sitting room eventually, armed with a tray.

'The coffee smells good,' he commented. 'Is there somewhere I could buy some brandy to go with it?'

'Yes, but you don't have to. Minerva's husband gave me two bottles of cognac for Christmas.'

James looked amused. 'You're that fond of it?'

'No, but Henry is. I ask them round for a meal every so often, so this is his way of saving me expense.'

'You like him.'

Rose nodded. 'Very much. Henry was a widower for years, and always the most determined of Minerva's men-friends. I'm glad she finally gave in and married him. And, far more important, so is she.'

'It must have been a surprise to her, all those years ago, when you told her *you* were married,' he commented.

'I never did tell her. At least not at the time.' Rose kept her eyes on the coffee she was pouring. 'Until last Sunday Minerva knew nothing about it. Henry's a solicitor, and I asked him to handle the divorce for me.' She looked up to meet the watchful, narrowed eyes. 'But before I could talk about divorce, of course, first I had to tell Minerva I was married.'

James whistled. 'That must have come as a shock after all this time.'

'It certainly did. Though Minerva always takes everything in her stride. She's the one person in this world,' said Rose deliberately, 'who I can trust to be there for me, no matter what.'

'Unlike me, you mean,' said James without expression, and took the coffee cup she handed him. 'If it's of any interest to you, Rose, I never told anyone about our marriage, either.'

'Not even your mother?'

'No one,' he repeated curtly. 'So what happened to break your silence after all this time?'

'Anthony asked me to marry him.' Rose shrugged. 'So I had to explain why that wasn't possible. I didn't tell him *why* I got married,' she added.

'Did you give your aunt the reason for our rush?'

'Yes.'

'But not Anthony.'

'No.'

He smiled a little. 'I'd forgotten how monosyllabic you get at times. Am I allowed to ask why you're keeping the man in the dark?'

Rose thought for a moment. 'I see no reason to tell him something which happened in the past, long before I met him.'

'Have you known him long?'

'I knew him by sight when I was young. But the present arrangement started a couple of months ago.'

'Do you love him?' probed James.

Rose looked away. 'I'm—fond of him.'

'That isn't what I asked.'

'Would you like more coffee?'

'In other words I should mind my own business,' he said wryly. 'But yes, I would like more coffee.'

Rose refilled their cups, aware that the truthful answer

to James's question was in the negative. Not that her feelings for Anthony Garrett, or any other man she knew, were anything to do with James Sinclair.

James took his coffee from her then sat down, his face sombre. 'I apologise. I've no right to intrude on your private affairs.'

She shrugged it off casually. 'Let's have some of Henry's cognac.' She gave him a wry look. 'Have you had dinner, by the way?'

James looked amused. 'Yes. Have *you* eaten, Rose?'

'Rather well, as it happens, a very conventional meat and potatoes kind of meal for once. Not that I bother with that kind of thing often. Normally it's just a salad, or—'

'Bacon sandwiches?'

Not for the world would Rose have told him that the very idea of a bacon sandwich had been anathema to her from the day they'd parted.

'I took a chance when I decided to knock on your door,' he said, as Rose poured brandy for him. 'But I was pretty sure that if I'd rung first you'd refuse to see me.'

'Why should you think that? I contacted you first.'

'But only by letter, which you signed very formally as Rose Dryden. You refused to speak to me often enough in the past, remember.' The grey eyes took on a cold, metallic gleam. 'Our parting was so acrimonious that even after all these years I wondered if you'd slam the door in my face tonight.'

Her chin lifted. 'I've grown up a bit since we last met, James.'

'You have, indeed.' He gazed at her thoughtfully. 'You know, Rose, I've often thought of how it would be if we met again.'

So had she. 'But obviously this isn't the scenario you pictured.'

'No. I assumed it would be in court, or some lawyer's office.'

'I'm surprised you came here in person, then.'

James shrugged. 'I acted on impulse. I was long over-due for a break, a colleague of mine knows this area well, so after I got your letter I decided on a trip to the Cotswolds.'

Rose raised an eyebrow. 'I'm surprised. The letter was pure formality. I didn't expect a reply, let alone the honour of a personal visit.'

James gave her a very unsettling smile. 'I decided it would be interesting to meet you just once again, Rose, before our lives are officially detached. A whim, I suppose. Only keep that fact to yourself. Professionally I'm not famous for whimsy.'

'Guarding your street cred again,' she said without thinking.

'Like another memorable occasion. No wonder you thought I sent you the card and the rose again,' he said, with an indulgence which irritated Rose considerably.

'Only for the briefest of moments,' she lied, and frowned. 'I just wish I knew who had.'

'But if someone's buying roses locally, surely you can find out?'

Rose explained how the first rose was ordered. 'But the second one could have been bought anywhere.'

James frowned. 'This is obviously getting to you, Rose. Have you no idea at all who could be doing this?'

'I did wonder if it was someone I knew in my time in London,' confessed Rose after a pause.

'What were you doing in London?'

Trying hard to forget James Sinclair, thought Rose with secret rancour. 'The usual things,' she told him. 'Earning a living, acquiring a succession of boyfriends. For a very brief time I even shared a flat with one of them—just before Minerva made me the offer I couldn't refuse. At which point the relationship came to an abrupt end.'

'Because you opted for the business?'

'Right. Rob had apparently been expecting me to marry him.'

'You didn't want that?'

'No.' Rose looked at him steadily. 'Oddly enough the encounter with you, James, put me off marriage for good.'

His mouth tightened. 'You've changed your mind now, obviously.'

'Actually, I haven't.' Rose shrugged. 'But Anthony's very conventional.'

'I see.' James swirled the brandy in his glass thoughtfully. 'Where's he based?'

'London,' she said, after a pause.

'In that case won't there be a conflict of interests again?' He raised an eyebrow. 'Something tells me this Anthony of yours doesn't really know very much about you, Rose. Have you talked this through?'

'Not yet. He mentioned marriage for the first time only last week.'

'But you obviously like the idea or you wouldn't have contacted me about the divorce.'

It had been dawning on Rose all evening that she'd made a very bad mistake in writing to James Sinclair instead of just instructing Henry to do it for her. His unexpected presence, here on her own private territory, was disturbing in the extreme.

'It merely nudged me into doing something I should have done long ago,' she said curtly. 'I'll make more coffee.'

Alone in her small kitchen, Rose faced the truth. There was no point in pretending she felt only indifference towards James Sinclair. Just having him in the same room smacked of danger. Even at twenty-two James had been a mature adult compared with the other students she'd known. But ten years on from that he was a formidable man who, as far as Rose could tell, still harboured resentment towards her. So before he caused any more damage to her life she needed to send him on his way, complete with an apology for any wrongs he felt she'd dealt him. Then both of them could get on with their lives, free of any emotional clutter left over from the past.

When she rejoined him, James watched in silence as she refilled their coffee cups.

'Before you leave, James, I'd like to get one thing straight,' Rose looked at him steadily. 'I didn't lie to you. I truly believed I was pregnant.'

'I know that,' he said, surprising her.

'You didn't believe me back then.'

'I've had a lot of time to think in the intervening years.'

'You said you haven't thought of me much.'

He smiled crookedly. 'Economy with the truth. I have my pride.'

'So have I.' Rose looked him in the eye. 'You hurt me badly, James. But at least I've matured enough to realise I hurt you equally as much.'

'More,' he contradicted. 'I was so crazy about you I wouldn't listen at first when that little reptile told me you set out to trap me. But then you admitted it was true, worse still told me there was no baby, and my world just fell apart. One minute you were the sweetest thing on God's earth; the next you seemed like the most conniving little witch I'd ever had the bad luck to encounter.'

Her eyes flashed. 'So you told me at the time. With colourful repetition.'

He winced. 'I'm not proud of the way I behaved, be-

lieve me. But I was so cut to pieces I hurled every insult
at you I could think of, and took off to Scotland to cool
off while you sat your exams. But you were my wife,
Rose. It never occurred to me that you'd vanish into thin
air by the time I got back.'

'I was obeying orders,' she reminded him. 'You told
me to get lost, so I did. Right out of the country for the
entire summer. When I came back Minerva told me you'd
rung quite a lot, so I said you were a boyfriend I'd
dumped, and if you rang again she was to say I wanted
nothing more to do with you.' Rose's mouth twisted in
self-derision. 'My own form of hubris, I suppose. Which
didn't do me much good when I went back to college.'

His eyes softened. 'Was it difficult for you?'

'Difficult! A few months as the legendary Sinclair's
girlfriend had boosted *my* street cred a sight too much.
For a while I was hounded by men panting to find out
what you found so special about me.'

'And did any of them succeed?'

Rose gave him a scathing look. 'Certainly not.
Eventually even the persistent Miles got the message. My
great good fortune was having two friends like Cornelia
Longford and Fabia Dennison. They knew nothing about
the wedding, of course, but Con, in particular, felt desperately responsible because you dumped me the minute
you found out about her famous plan. I had to seem to
get over you just to reassure her. So in time I did.'

'How much time?' he demanded.

'At lot more than I would have liked.'

James nodded. 'Likewise.'

'But you had your job in the City, and a whole new
life. I doubt that you thought of me for long,' she said
scornfully.

'I did my thinking at night. In bed.' His eyes met hers. 'We were very good together, Rose.'

So good that she'd never found anyone to take his place, thought Rose, suppressing a shiver. She'd thought for a while she'd succeeded with Robert Mason. Until marriage had been mentioned.

Rose jumped to her feet. 'I'm sorry to be rude, James, but it's getting late and my day starts early.' She smiled politely. 'At least it isn't much of a walk for you to the King's Head.'

'I'm not putting up there.'

She frowned. 'But you said you walked.'

'I did. The colleague I mentioned owns a weekend place, a cottage down by the river. It's a fine evening. I was glad of the exercise.' James smiled as he stood up. 'I'm there for a few days for some much needed R and R. You look surprised, Rose.'

Dismayed, not surprised. 'How pleasant,' she said politely. 'I'm sure you'll enjoy it there.'

He took his wallet from his jacket, extracted a business card and scribbled a number on it. 'There's no phone at the cottage, but you can reach me on my cellphone number any time you need to. Let me know if your stalker steps up his attentions.'

'Thank you,' said Rose.

They were almost at the door when James stopped suddenly, and held out his hand. 'Ten years ago, Rose, I said a great many things I would have given a lot to retract afterwards. I can't take them back, but at least I can tell you how much I've regretted them since. I know the apology's long overdue, but I'm sorry I hurt you so badly.'

With reluctance Rose put her hand in his, wary even now of touching him. 'Apology accepted. It was all a long time ago. Let's put it all behind us.'

'There's a snag,' said James, in a tone that quickened her pulse. 'Now I've seen you again it doesn't feel like a long time ago.'

'Nevertheless,' Rose said woodenly, 'it is. But now we've made our apologies at last, and washed away any bitterness.' Which came out sounding a lot more biblical than intended. But it was impossible to behave, or sound, natural when the mere touch of James Sinclair's hand on hers was rousing feelings she had never experienced in the most passionate of lovemaking with anyone else.

And James knew it, she realised, as she met the blaze of triumph in his eyes.

'Rose.' He smiled slowly, and brushed a lock of hair back from her face. 'Surely a kiss goodbye is permissible in the circumstances?' He drew her resisting body into his arms and kissed her, taking his time over it, the shape and taste and touch of his lips so frighteningly familiar she had no defence against the hot, consuming pleasure of the kiss. When the phone interrupted stridently, bringing her back to earth, she wrenched away to answer it, but James grabbed her hand, shaking his head. He snatched up the receiver and snarled a response.

Rose waited, tense, as he listened for a second.

'Who the hell is this?' James demanded roughly. 'Who-ever you are you can stop your game right now. I've in-formed the police, so this call is being traced as we speak—' He broke off, lips twitching as he listened. 'Ah! I see. Sorry. Of course. I'll hand you over right now.'

'Who the devil was that?' howled Anthony in Rose's ear.

'I've been getting anonymous phone calls,' she said breathlessly, avoiding amused grey eyes. 'James assumed you were the culprit.'

'And who, may I ask, is James?'

'He called to discuss the divorce.'

There was a pause. 'Are you talking about your *husband*?' said Anthony in outrage. 'Why the blazes did you invite him to your place?'

'I didn't do that,' she retorted, struggling to keep her temper. 'Anyway, I can't talk now, Anthony. I'll—I'll ring you later.' She put the phone down to find James eavesdropping shamelessly.

'Sorry about that, Rose,' he said, shrugging. 'I heard dead silence on the line for a minute—'

'Shock at hearing a man where Anthony least expected one,' said Rose tightly.

'I thought it was your stalker. I hope I haven't made things difficult for you,' James added, with such patent insincerity Rose clenched her teeth.

'Not at all,' she said crisply. 'I'll show you out.' She marched down the steep flight of stairs ahead of him. 'I'm glad we've cleared things up at last. Henry will keep you up to speed on the divorce. Goodbye, James.'

'Wait.' He stood close in the small lobby, his eyes intent on hers. 'Will you really be happy, Rose?'

She dropped her eyes. 'My life is nothing to do with you any more.'

He smiled slowly. 'After meeting you again I somehow find it hard to get my head round that. Goodnight,' he added, a caressing note in his voice which made Rose unwilling to trust her own as she opened the door to let him out.

'Lock up securely,' James ordered, as he went out into the cobbled street. 'Disconnect your phone and get some rest.'

Easier said than done, thought Rose, almost tearful with resentment as she got ready for bed. After years of believing she was over James Sinclair, the discovery that she was anything but was no preparation for a good night's sleep. She was an adult now, for heaven's sake, not a starry-eyed teenager to be bowled over by a kiss. Rose groaned in despair. Divorcing James Sinclair might be easy enough, but trying to forget she'd ever been married to him would be harder than ever now she'd met up with him again.

CHAPTER NINE

ROSE felt on edge all next day, half expecting to see James Sinclair walk in every time the shop door opened. But when there was no sign of him by the time she locked up at five-thirty, she shut herself in her office, mortified by her own disappointment.

As punishment for her absurdity she forced herself to do twice her usual session of paperwork, then had a shower and dressed in faded old jeans and yellow sweatshirt, but paid close attention to hair and face afterwards, just in case James reappeared on her doorstep later.

Rose tidied her sitting room at top speed, threw a salad together, switched on her television and sat down on the sofa to eat her supper, with one of the newest arrivals on the bestseller list beside her. If James did come—not that she really thought for a moment that he would, of course—she would convey the perfect picture of someone enjoying a cosy evening, perfectly happy with her own company.

She had barely started on her salad when her private doorbell rang, and a triumphant smile curved her mouth as she pushed the tray aside. Elation surged inside her as she ran downstairs, then evaporated sharply when she opened the door.

'Anthony!' exclaimed Rose.

He eyed her truculently. 'I waited up for hours for you to ring me back last night. When you didn't I decided to make a personal visit today instead. May I come in, or would I be intruding?'

'No you wouldn't,' she said crisply, and turned to go ahead of him up the stairs. 'I was in the middle of supper. Shall I make some for you?'

'No, thanks,' he said, his mood lightening when he spotted a tray very obviously laid for one. 'Marcus is meeting me at Orsini's for dinner shortly. But you carry on with your meal, of course.'

'It won't spoil. I'll eat it later.' In peace, she almost added. 'You didn't tell me you were coming tonight.'

'I drove down on impulse,' he said quickly.

Other people's impulses were playing havoc with her life at the moment, thought Rose irritably, and gave her visitor a sweet little smile. 'Are you taking a chance on having your room free tonight at the Kings Head, then?'

'I rang them first to make sure,' he admitted, flushing. 'I knew you'd be busy in the shop so I didn't bother to interrupt with a phone call.'

But he'd rung Marcus. And booked a meal at Orsini's. So Anthony had obviously called on her unannounced because he'd hoped, or feared, to catch her entertaining James. 'I might not have been in,' she pointed out.

'In which case I would have rung from the hotel and left a message on your machine,' he said, after a pause that convinced Rose he'd only just thought of it.

'So,' she said briskly, 'is there a specific reason for seeing me tonight, Anthony?'

'Yes, a very important one.' He stood very erect, squaring his shoulders in a mannerism Rose knew well. 'I came to let you know I've engaged my own solicitor, so you needn't worry your head about it any more. Emerson will see to the divorce proceedings.'

Rose stared him in outrage. '*What* did you say?'

His eyes flickered. 'I've simply set the ball rolling for you.'

Her eyes flashed ominously. 'I can't believe you did that without consulting me, Anthony.'

His chin came up. 'It seemed to me you'd go on shilly-shallying indefinitely if I didn't take a hand in it. Anyway, it's all settled with Emerson now—'

'Then get it unsettled,' she snapped. 'I'm putting everything in Henry Beresford's hands on Monday.'

'Henry's semi-retired,' said Anthony impatiently. 'Besides, he's not experienced in divorce. Emerson will get it sorted out far more quickly.'

'Not in my case,' said Rose, ice dripping from every word. 'I wouldn't dream of hurting Henry, which, in case you've forgotten, would also hurt Minerva. In fact, Anthony, I deeply resent your interference.'

His colour deepened hectically. 'I meant it as *help*, Rose, not interference.'

'Really! And when, exactly, did you decide to consult this Mr Emerson?'

'Today. Though I don't see the relevance—'

'Do you think I'm stupid, Anthony?' Rose eyed him with scorn. 'You discovered that James was here last night and acted on another of these impulses of yours.'

'All right! Now you've brought the subject up, what exactly was he doing here?' demanded Anthony, a vein standing out on his temple. 'Do you expect me to believe that after ten years he just turned up on your doorstep out of the blue?'

Rose looked at him in distaste. 'I don't expect you to believe anything.'

'So you were lying—'

'I am not lying,' she said, with such icy emphasis Anthony Garrett backed away a little.

'I'm sorry,' he said, raking a hand through his hair.

Which showed Rose how upset he was. Anthony was particular about his hair.

'You'd better go,' she said coldly. 'Otherwise you'll be late for Marcus.'

'Look, I admit I went about this the wrong way. We'll discuss it tomorrow night, Rose.' He smiled cajolingly. 'I'll take you up on your recent offer of dinner here instead of going out.'

'Certainly not!'

'All right,' he said quickly, looking crestfallen, 'let's keep to a meal at Orsini's, then, and talk over coffee here later.'

Rose sighed impatiently. 'You don't understand, Anthony. I can't see you at all tomorrow.'

He glowered at her. 'Are you doing this just to punish me over the solicitor?'

'It's part of it. But I also resent the fact that you assume I'm at your beck and call just because you take it into your head to come down this weekend,' she said hotly, then tensed at the look of rage on his face.

'It's this husband of yours, isn't it?' he demanded. 'You're seeing *him* tomorrow, I suppose!'

'Don't be childish,' said Rose, and regretted it when Anthony seized her by the shoulders and shook her so hard her teeth rattled.

'You were lying when you said you hadn't seen him all this time,' he snarled. 'After ten years he suddenly turns up last night? Do you think I'm a fool? No doubt you slept with him for old times' sake—'

'Let her go,' rapped a hard, frozen voice.

'And who the hell are you?' said Anthony in outrage, his hands tightening on Rose's shoulders as he glared at the tall man standing in the doorway.

'I think you know very well who I am. My name's

Sinclair. Take your hands off my wife.' James shook his head at Rose. 'You shouldn't leave your door ajar. Any riff-raff could have got in. And obviously did.'

Scarlet to the roots of his hair, Anthony Garrett clenched the hands he'd dropped from Rose's shoulders, so patently wanting to hit James that Rose felt a fleeting pang of sympathy for his frustration. But something in James's attitude warned that her enraged assailant would do well to make himself scarce.

'You'd better go, Anthony,' she advised.

'Very well.' He pulled himself together with difficulty. 'I'll—I'll ring you tomorrow, Rose. When you're in a more reasonable frame of mind.'

'I'll see you out,' she said promptly, but James put out a peremptory hand.

'No. Stay where you are, Rose. I'll see your visitor off the premises. And make sure your door's locked securely while I'm at it.'

Rose slumped down on the sofa as her visitors went downstairs. She tried to make out what was being said, but all was ominously quiet before the outer door banged shut.

'Are you all right, Rose?' said James, when he rejoined her.

'Yes.' She rubbed at her shoulders, smiling ruefully. 'A bit bruised, but otherwise suffering mainly from temper.'

'Because the bastard manhandled you?'

'No. Though I didn't care for that very much, either.' Her eyes flashed coldly. 'Anthony made a colossal mistake today. He actually engaged his own solicitor to see to the divorce. Without consulting me.'

'Brave man!' James sat down beside her, eyeing her closely. 'You objected?'

'Of course I objected,' she retorted. 'I refuse to be pushed into anything.'

His eyes gleamed. 'So you're not as keen on the idea of divorce as your friend believes?'

Her chin lifted. 'On the contrary. I'm very keen on it indeed. But my aunt's husband handles all my legal affairs, so naturally I'll ask Henry to see to the divorce.' She frowned. 'That was a rather dramatic appearance just now, by the way. What brings you here again so soon, James?'

'I happened to be passing—' He grinned at the scathing look she gave him and raised his right hand. 'I was, I swear. I booked dinner at the Italian restaurant and I was quite literally on my way past your shop when I saw your private door was ajar. So mindful of your stalker, I came rushing to your rescue. And not before time, either,' he added grimly. 'Your friend looked ready to do you a mischief.'

'He was just jealous,' said Rose dismissively.

James sat back, arms folded, looking smug. 'Of me?'

'Yes. He didn't take kindly to your presence here last night.'

He smiled evilly. 'He didn't take very kindly to it tonight, either.'

'Do you blame him? For a moment there I thought you were going to knock him down.'

'So did I.' James shook his head in wonder. 'It's not a habit of mine to go round throwing punches, but I came very close with your little friend.'

'James!' protested Rose. 'Anthony's not *little*.'

'He's smaller than me.' He sighed regretfully. 'Which meant I couldn't indulge myself by throwing him down your stairs.'

'Are you into violence a lot these days?'

'No. And in the past only on your behalf, if you recall.'

'I can fight my own battles, thanks just the same.' She looked at her abandoned supper. 'What time's your reservation?'

'Half an hour ago.'

'Ring them and explain.'

James eyed her tray disparagingly. 'I've got a better idea. I know there's no point in asking you to keep me company at the restaurant, but they do food to take out. Ask them to send dinner for two here.' He smiled into her startled eyes. 'No one will know exactly *who* you're entertaining, Rose.'

'True. But at Orsini's they'll know who I'm *not* entertaining. Anthony's dining there tonight with his son.'

'Public opinion has always been such a huge thing with you,' he said impatiently. 'At university I had to make a total spectacle of myself before you'd agree to let the world know we were—'

'Going out together.'

'Only we didn't go out very much.'

'Better if we had,' said Rose bleakly.

James changed tack. 'Right. If you won't go out, and you won't order anything in, there's a third option.'

She eyed him suspiciously. 'What is it?'

'Come down to the cottage and I'll cater for you there.'

Rose's first reaction was to refuse. Last night was meant to be a one-off, she reminded herself, since James Sinclair represented such a clear and present danger to her peace of mind. But she was sorely tempted by his offer, just the same. After the excitement of the past half-hour an evening on her own would be anticlimax. She smiled a little. 'Is having dinner together accepted behaviour for people about to divorce?'

He shrugged. 'No idea. Your letter started me on a bit

of research to get up to date on the subject, but I don't remember any veto on a friendly evening spent in each other's company.' His eyes locked with hers. 'We were good friends, once, Rose. Did I alienate you too much, all those years ago, for us to be friends again?'

She met the look head-on. 'I certainly thought you had at the time.'

'Do you still feel the same?'

Rose shook her head. 'Ten years is a long time to nourish hatred. I couldn't sustain the emotion indefinitely so I concentrated on forgetting you instead.'

'I hope you succeeded better than I did.' His mouth twisted. 'When I finally calmed down enough to engage my brain all those years ago I soon realised the truth of what you told me last night. No one can *make* someone else fall in love. I rushed back from Scotland to tell you that, to say that I loved my little wife so much I didn't care why we'd got married as long as we stayed that way. But the bird had flown.'

'To look after a couple of toddlers for the rest of the summer,' said Rose huskily, and looked away, not wanting him to see how much his words had moved her. 'It takes a lot of energy to look after children all day. I was so tired most nights I fell asleep the moment I got to bed.' Which told him she hadn't lain sleepless, agonising over the treatment he'd dished out, for the simple reason that she'd made very sure she was too exhausted to stay awake.

'By that time I'd been accepted by the bank I joined straight from college,' said James, watching her like a hawk. 'Which was another reason why I went rushing back to you. I wanted to share my pleasure in getting my first job. Maybe you didn't realise it, Rose, but when your aunt eventually told me you wanted nothing more to do with me, you had your revenge in full.'

'Exactly as I intended.' Rose shivered suddenly. 'But I don't want to drag all that up again. Let's change the subject.'

'Done. Come and spend the evening at the cottage. It's very peaceful on that stretch of river.' He got to his feet, his eyes gleaming in a way that did serious damage to her heartbeat. 'All you're agreeing to is a scratch meal, Rose, and a couple of hours of catching up on our lives.'

'Why not?' she said casually, ignoring fierce urgings of caution from her brain. 'I'll drive; you give directions. I haven't been down that way for years. It's a long time since I went walking by the river with Mark Cummings.'

'Does this mean you're actually willing to be seen in my company as far as the public car park?' said James caustically.

'No.' Rose gave him a seraphic smile. 'There's a back door in the store room behind my office. My car's parked just outside.'

'So you can smuggle me out with no one the wiser!'

She bristled. 'Amusing though it may be to you, James, I don't keep my car in the back for secrecy. Like everyone else with a shop in the arcade here, it's merely the most convenient place to park.'

The small, stone-built cottage James directed her to was reached by a narrow track leading off a road so minor they almost missed it in the dark.

'I had a hell of a job finding it the first time,' he said, as Rose came to a stop beside the house. 'There were no lights on like this when I arrived, so even with the map I drove past several times in the dark before I made it. But if you want peace and quiet this is certainly the place to come.'

'Is that why you came here?'

'No. I came to see you.' James unlocked a door beneath a stone lintel, and ushered Rose into a welcoming, lamp-lit room with an inglenook fireplace. A laptop sat on a large leather-topped desk beneath the front window, and the chairs and sofa grouped around the room were well-worn and comfortable.

'This is lovely,' said Rose, as James stooped to light the fire.

'To add a little cheer,' he announced, as realistic flames danced on equally realistic logs.

'Not town gas as far out as this, surely,' said Rose.

'Bottled.' James grinned. 'Nick's wife likes the look of a fire, but not the mess that goes with it.'

'She doesn't object to the isolation?'

'No. They're still at the honeymoon stage. They both work hard during the week, and escape down here when-ever they can just to be together in peace. Like most nor-mal newly-weds,' he added deliberately.

'We were studying too hard to be normal newly-weds,' said Rose, refusing to rise. 'Our marriage was only on paper. We never did live together properly.'

Once James had organised a licence they'd been mar-ried very early one wet May morning at a register office, with only cleaners for witnesses. Afterwards the bride-groom had rushed off to sit an exam and the bride had returned, alone and disconsolate, to her college flat. Their nearest thing to a honeymoon had been spent beforehand, during the Easter vacation, when James had taken her to stay for a week in the Lake District, in a cottage not unlike this one. It had rained so much most of their time had been spent in bed.

'It amazes me,' he said, after a while, 'that you never told your aunt we were married.'

'There didn't seem much point. If you remember, I was adamant about keeping it from any of our friends at the time—'

'Of course I remember,' he said scornfully. 'You were so hysterical about your secret I felt like a murderer.'

Rose eyed him uncertainly. 'What do you mean?'

'Can't you imagine how guilty I felt about getting you pregnant? How the responsibility of it all weighed down like a ton?' His mouth twisted. 'I couldn't even enjoy the privileges of any normal bridegroom because I was working like a maniac—spurred on to do well in my finals so I could get a job good enough to support you and the baby.'

Rose had never looked past the rage and humiliation of their last meeting to consider this point of view. 'I caused you a whole lot of trouble, didn't I?' she said after a while.

James smiled a little. 'Not all trouble. All right, if you hadn't embarked on this famous plan of yours I probably wouldn't have noticed you. But the fact remains that when I did I fell crazily in love with you. I had no objection at all to marrying you, Rose, ever. Only the reason for the rush.'

'Fatherhood thrust upon you and all that,' she said sadly.

'No,' he said forcibly, and put a finger under her chin to turn her face up to his. 'I was appalled because I'd forced motherhood on *you*.'

Rose returned the look steadily. 'There wasn't much forcing about it, James. I was very much in love, too. Which is why—'

'Why I hurt you so badly,' he finished for her.

'But hurt heals. And I'm not in love with you any more,' she said flatly, 'so let's forget the past.'

James studied her face at length, with a look far too much like a jungle cat about to pounce on its prey for Rose's liking. 'Right. If the past is taboo we'll discuss supper instead, Miss Dryden—' He stopped, smiling crookedly.

'Keep to Rose,' she advised, determinedly prosaic. 'And lead me to the fridge. It's long past my suppertime. I need food.'

The galley kitchen was very modern, and very small, and James refused to let Rose set foot in it.

'There's no room for two of us. I promised you dinner, so I shall provide it,' he said firmly. 'You sit down in front of the fire and relax with a book, just as you were doing earlier on before the fun started.'

'An offer I can't refuse! Sitting down is my favourite pastime after a day on my feet.' Rose left James to his labour and retreated to the sitting room, where alcoves with well-stocked bookshelves offered literature very much to her taste, as long as she was happy with something she'd read before.

She chose a worn volume of Jane Austen's *Persuasion*, and curled up in the corner of the sofa, her eyes on the man-made flames. She read a page or two, then stiffened as the scent of grilling bacon came drifting from the kitchen. Not the famous sandwiches! Surely James had more subtlety than that.

Rose soon found that he had. In a remarkably short time she was provided with a plateful of pasta mixed with diced pancetta and tangy tomato sauce.

'Thank you! I'm impressed. How on earth did you manage all this so quickly?'

'I brought a few basics with me.' James put a glass of

wine on the table beside her. 'But Becky Henstridge's store cupboard provided the sauce and the pasta. And Nick keeps a fair selection of wine on hand.'

'Do you cook for yourself a lot?'

'No more than I have to. I eat out, or get a meal sent in.'

'When I smelt the pancetta cooking I thought I was getting one of your celebrated bacon sandwiches,' Rose informed him.

His jaw tightened. 'My enthusiasm for those vanished the day you left me.'

Suddenly all pretence of harmony was gone. They went on with the meal in silence, the remembrance of things past raw in the air between them.

'I've often thought of contacting you again, Rose,' said James after a while. 'Then I'd remember how you refused to speak to me, and my ego baulked at the idea of more rejection.'

While she, unable to accept that all was over between them, had watched for every post, and tensed every time the phone rang once she was back in college, or even at home, in spite of her instructions to Minerva.

Rose smiled politely, and pushed her plate away. 'I'm afraid you were over-generous, James. This is delicious, but I can't eat any more.'

He got up at once and took their plates into the kitchen, then came back with a bottle wrapped in a napkin. 'You haven't touched your wine yet,' he pointed out as he re-filled his glass.

She sipped obediently, and smiled. 'I never developed much of a palate, but this is wonderful. Is it a *rosé*?'

James lips twitched. 'Close.'

'What, then?'

He removed the napkin to reveal a staggeringly expensive brand of pink champagne. 'Don't worry, I'll replace it before I go. But in the circumstances it seemed an appropriate choice to celebrate our reunion. I always hoped that one day we'd be in contact again, over the divorce if nothing else.' His smile clenched her stomach muscles. 'Old flames are normally easy to put out the minute the affair is over. But you and I were actually married, Rose, which made you a tad harder to extinguish than the others.'

How many others? wondered Rose, giving him a hostile look. 'You could have divorced me any time you wanted, James.'

'I've explained my reasons for being quite happy with the status quo,' he reminded her blandly. 'But let's not waste time on recriminations. This kind of occasion can hardly be repeated now you're thinking of marrying again. What's the man's surname, by the way? Referring to him as Anthony sounds too damn friendly on my part.'

'Garrett,' said Rose, digesting the fact that this evening was to be a one-off in the lives of James and Rose Sinclair. What had she expected? she thought impatiently, astonished to find a lump in her throat at the thought of the name she'd never used. Rose Sinclair sounded so utterly right. But it was no use thinking of that now. After tonight she might never be in touch with James again, other than through a solicitor. She finished her champagne hurriedly, and James got up to refill her glass.

'I shouldn't,' she said with regret. 'I'm driving.'

'It's a very quiet road back. I doubt you'll meet a policeman desperate to breathalise you. Besides,' he added, 'two glasses of wine won't do much harm.'

'I know. That's my usual allowance when I'm wining and dining.'

'With Garrett, of course.'

'Not exclusively. I get asked out to dinner parties some-times, and I enjoy the occasional date with one of the solicitors in Henry's chambers. And I often make up a four with Mark and Bel Cummings and her man.'

James's eyes narrowed. 'The name Cummings rings a bell.'

Rose nodded. 'Mark was my first boyfriend. He teaches history at his old school. He's a single parent now, with a small daughter he's bringing up with help from his mother and Bel, and even me, sometimes, when he's stuck for a babysitter.'

'What happened to his wife?'

'She took off with someone else before Lucy learned to walk.'

James gave her a searching look. 'Was that before you came back to take over the bookshop?'

'Long before.'

'Cummings must have welcomed you back to the fold with open arms, then.'

'Yes, he did. We're old friends.'

'Does he know about me?'

'No.' She gave him a taunting little smile. 'Everyone has a skeleton in the cupboard, James. You're mine.'

'Nothing's changed, then,' he said curtly. 'I assume I can't tempt you to more champagne?'

'No, thanks.'

James poured the last of the wine into his glass, looking down into it with a brooding look Rose remembered well. 'So when are you going to come out of the closet, Rose, and tell the world you've been a married lady all along?'

'I don't imagine the world is all that interested!'

'I meant this pretty little town of yours.'

'I don't expect anything more than the merest ripple of interest,' said Rose firmly. 'No one knows *you* here. And

I was quite respectably—if briefly—your wife; nothing remotely newsworthy.'

'You still *are* my wife,' James reminded her, his eyes clashing with hers.

She looked away. 'Only in the eyes of the law.'

'I wonder how it would have been,' he said musingly, 'if we'd stayed together.'

Rose shrugged carelessly. 'Who knows? The marriage success rate's not very high these days, and we were very young. We would probably have split up long before now.'

'Do you really believe that, Rose?' he said, startling her.

She gave him a long, analytical look. Seeing James Sinclair as he was now, even more attractive in her eyes than before, it was hard to believe that she would have ever left him willingly. 'I don't know,' she said honestly. 'Nor does it matter. It's all academic now.'

'If you say so. Tell me,' added James, 'having met the man, I can't believe you really want to marry Garrett, Rose. You must have other reasons for wanting a divorce.'

She frowned. 'What do you mean?'

'This Mark Cummings. It seems to me he's in need of a wife and a mother for his child. Has he cast you in the role?'

'Heavens, I hope not,' said Rose involuntarily.

'You don't care for the idea?'

'No. And not,' she added tartly, 'because I'm still married to you, either. I just don't care for Mark that way. Besides, I think he still lives in hope that his wife will go back to him some day.'

His mouth twisted. 'I can understand that.'

Her eyes flew to his in astonishment.

'For a long time after you left me,' James told her, his eyes locked with hers, 'I hoped we'd get together again.'

'Did you?' she said huskily.

James nodded. 'I even came here to Chastlecombe, determined to mend things between us. And caught sight of you walking down the street with a stocky, fair-haired man. You were laughing together, and so obviously a pair I dodged out of sight. After that I felt fate was telling me to give up. I didn't try again.'

Rose stared at him wordlessly, feeling her heart contract. 'It must have been Mark. How strange.' She dropped her eyes to hide sudden moisture on her lashes.

James turned her face up to his. 'Don't, Rose. That's the way I've remembered you all these years, in floods of tears during that gut-wrenching fight just before we split up. This time I want a happier picture for a keepsake.'

'I'm not crying,' she assured him, and smiled crookedly. 'Just mourning for what might have been.'

'It doesn't have to be in the past tense,' he said with sudden force, and pulled her out of the chair and into his arms. He tipped her face up to his, his eyes glittering with a heat that made her tremble. 'Look me in the eye, Rose Sinclair, and tell me you feel absolutely nothing for me.'

CHAPTER TEN

HELD so close to him, Rose knew there was no point in trying to lie. 'I can't do that,' she said, resentful of her body's treachery. 'Though, Lord knows, I'm entitled to feel enmity, James, if nothing else, after the things you once said to me. Which hurt all the more because some of them were true.' She looked up at him in appeal. 'Though in the beginning I didn't dream that Con's blueprint for seduction would succeed.'

'But it did—God, how it did,' he said bitterly. 'How I passed my exams I'll never know. All the time I was revising I just wanted to be with you, making love to my wife.'

'I followed orders faithfully—kept away from you the whole time,' she protested, wishing she had more control over her pulse.

'True. But just because you weren't there in the flesh—' He stopped, jaw clenched, and Rose swallowed hard, conscious that her breasts were hardening in response to his nearness, and a secret liquefying feeling lower down gave humiliating proof that James Sinclair still had the power to arouse her in ways no other man had ever done. And knew this only too well by the look in his eyes.

'Let me go, James,' she said quietly. *Please* let me go, she begged silently, before I do something I'm sure to regret later when you're gone.

'I don't want to let you go. I've always been curious to know if the chemistry would still be there. And it is.

136

Don't try to deny it.' His arms tightened instinctively. 'You owe me the truth.'

'I don't owe you anything!'

'Oh, yes, you do.' His eyes bored into hers. 'You're the reason I'm still on my own, lady. I've never been able to commit to the other women in my life because there you were in the background, reminding me of what happens when a man loses his head.'

'That's nothing to do with me,' she said, angry at the mention of other women.

'Of course it is.' He slid a hand down her cheek. 'I suppose I always knew what type of woman you'd become. You're not beautiful, but there's something about that face and body of yours that still gets to me like no other woman's ever has. Not that it matters to you now, of course,' he added suavely. 'Because you're not in love with me any more.'

'Exactly.' Rose shoved him away and stood back. 'Just how many women have there been, as a matter of interest?'

'It matters to you?' he demanded in triumph.

Oh, yes. It mattered.

'Of course it doesn't,' she assured him, and turned to pick up her glass. 'I was angry when I first saw you last night. But I'm not any longer. In fact I think it's a good thing we met up one last time to discuss the divorce in an adult, civilised way.'

'Civilised!' he growled, and snatched the glass away from her. 'I don't feel civilised, Rose. I don't know what there is about you that's so different from—'

'The others?'

He smiled slowly, and Rose quivered inside as he pulled her against him. 'Can you honestly say there's nothing happening between us? And,' he added, in a tone which turned her bones to jelly, 'I'm not discussing things cerebral here.'

Without waiting for a reply James ended the argument in the way he had ended many an argument between them in the past. His lips took possession of hers, parting them, urging a response, his seducing tongue sending heat rushing through her body. He scooped her up and sat down with her in his lap, enclosing her in the embrace she had missed as much his lovemaking once it was no longer part of her life.

'In that get-up you look like the teenager I was so crazy about. It's hard to realise ten years have elapsed, Rose.'

'But they have,' she said in alarm. 'And you promised this wouldn't happen!'

He smoothed her hair back, his eyes hot on hers. 'Nothing has happened. Yet.' He pulled her close to kiss her, one hand sliding down her back. 'I shouldn't have mentioned the word "flesh",' he said against her mouth.

'Very evocative word,' she agreed with difficulty as his exploring fingers played havoc with her resistance, his touch burning through her shirt.

'And if I am trying to seduce you, it's only fair.' He put a finger under her chin. 'Isn't that what you did to me all those years ago?'

Rose thrust him away. 'I never imagined for a moment that my plan would entail carnal knowledge of my quarry, Sinclair.'

He raised a cynical eyebrow. 'But isn't that what you intended?'

She shook her head. 'I never aimed so high—or do I mean low? The idea was to make you fall in love with me; that's all.'

'The two are not mutually exclusive! Once I'd kissed you all I could think of was teaching you everything I knew about the rest of it. I'm amazed I held off as long as I did.'

Rose gazed into his relentless eyes for a moment, then, summoning every shred of self-control she possessed, she stood up. 'Time I went home.'

His eyes hardened so suddenly she backed away as he leapt to his feet. 'You don't mean that, Rose.'

'I do, you know!'

His mouth twisted. 'Delayed retribution?'

'Nothing so dramatic. Just common sense.' She squared her shoulders. 'I'll be honest, James, and admit that part of me, the physical part, wants to give in to whatever you have in mind. But my brain tells me you can't walk back into my life after ten years and expect me to jump into bed with you at the snap of your fingers just because you fancy a little payback of some kind. I'm human enough to be flattered that you want me, of course.'

He leaned an elbow on the stone ledge above the fireplace. 'Are you still saying you feel nothing in return, Rose?'

'No,' she said unwillingly. 'But there are several reasons why I won't go to bed with you—'

'You mean make love with me.'

'For one thing,' she said, ignoring him, 'it could complicate the divorce.'

'Ah, yes, the divorce.' James's eyes narrowed to a predatory gleam. 'Tell me, Rose, what would happen if I informed your solicitor that I wanted a reconciliation?'

'This isn't something to joke about,' she snapped.

'Who says I'm joking?'

Rose turned away in angry defeat. 'It's too late for all this, James.'

'It's only a little before eleven, Rose.'

'I mean it's ten years too late.' She turned to face him. 'Or is all this just to queer Anthony Garrett's pitch?'

The surprise on James's face was genuine. 'I never gave him a thought,' he assured her. 'I don't think he's right for you, but if you tell me you love the man I'll never darken your door again. But you don't love him, Rose. And you know it.' He moved from the fireplace and took her by the shoulders, then dropped his hands, scowling when she flinched. 'The bastard hurt you—let me see.'

Rose slid the sweatshirt off one shoulder, craning to see the damage, then caught her breath as James laid his lips to the bruise, his tongue licking in deliberate caress as his hair brushed her skin.

'Don't worry,' he whispered, 'I'm just kissing it better.'

She covered herself hurriedly, and collected her bag. 'Goodnight, James. Thank you for dinner.'

'Wait.' James took her hand. 'When can I see you again?'

'I don't think that's a good idea, James.'

'Why not?'

Rose regarded him steadily. 'Because underneath all the blarney you're still angry with me, aren't you?'

'Do you blame me?'

'No. But it makes me uneasy. So it's best we say goodbye, James.'

'You've grown into a hard woman, Rose Sinclair,' he said, shaking his head.

'Don't call me that!'

'It's your name. In the eyes of the law you're still my legally wedded wife, remember.' His eyes held hers. 'If I'd carried you upstairs just now, as I wanted to, there would have been nothing against an old married couple sharing a bed together.'

'That's sophistry—' She turned away, unable to face

the mocking grey eyes a moment longer. 'And time I went. Thank you for dinner.'

He was frowning as he walked with her to the car. 'Rose, I'm not happy about your driving home alone. I'll come with you and walk back. Or I can just follow you in my car until I know you're safe.'

'Thank you, but no,' she said decisively. 'I can't go on jumping at shadows, James. And I have to live here after you're long gone, remember.'

'But I haven't gone yet, so ring me as soon as you get home and confirm you're safe and sound.'

'All right. I will. But I warn you, I'm a slow, cautious driver.' Rose smiled up at him, then drove off quickly, before James discovered how much she wanted to stay.

Rose parked her car in its usual niche behind the shop, let herself in through the back door and turned on the hall light. And found another rose lying inside her private door.

She raced upstairs, and rang James's cellphone number with a shaking hand. 'I'm home,' she said tersely. 'But I don't feel safe and sound. Another rose was waiting for me.'

James cursed colourfully. 'Rose, call the police right now,' he ordered.

'Not tonight. I'm tired; I need to go to bed. I'll call them tomorrow.'

'Then I'll come and sleep on your sofa—'

'No way, James.' No point in exchanging one danger for another. 'I'll be fine now. Everything's locked, bolted or disconnected. All I have to do is get myself to bed.'

'All right, have it your own way,' he said impatiently. 'But ring me if the least thing disturbs you. However late it is. And give me your cellphone number so I can check on you in the morning. Are you seeing Garrett tomorrow night, by the way?'

'No way! He wasn't due to come down this weekend. I was so furious with him about the solicitor I turned him down flat when he took it for granted I'd be available just because he was.'

'This man hasn't got a clue where you're concerned!' James paused. 'Look, Rose, now I'm here I want to see you again before the law separates us for good. I assume there's no point in asking you to go out somewhere, so come here for a meal again tomorrow. Look on it as a kind of farewell party, if you like.'

Rose hesitated. Another evening in that cosy, isolated cottage would be asking for trouble. But there was no point in deluding herself. She wanted—needed—to see James again. Just one last time. But here on home ground, on her own territory. 'Come and have dinner here, instead,' she said casually.

There was dead silence for a moment. 'With the greatest of pleasure,' said James, openly surprised. 'Do I slink from the car park in disguise?'

'No. Just arrive brazenly at my door as usual. About eight?'

'Eight it is. Rose,' he added swiftly, 'do you feel better now?'

'Yes, I do.' The mere sound of James's voice had dispelled her panic. 'Goodnight.'

Before disconnecting her phone Rose listened to three consecutive messages from Anthony, begging her to change her mind about their Saturday night arrangement.

No chance, thought Rose, as she got ready for bed. Whatever happened from now on, Anthony Garrett was history. She put him from her mind and thought about

James at length instead, and eventually slept until the phone on the pillow beside her woke her up.

'Good morning,' said James. 'Did you sleep?'

'Gosh, you're early.' Rose yawned, peering at her watch. 'Amazingly enough I slept very well.'

'While I tossed and turned in my cold and lonely bed,' he said, sighing.

'How sad!'

'Unsympathetic creature. Now then, Rose,' he added, suddenly businesslike, 'phone the police this morning.'

'No. It's exactly the sort of publicity I could do without. And in broad daylight it just seems silly. No actual crime has been committed. It's not against the law to send roses.'

'I don't like it, just the same.'

'Neither do I. But if I ignore it, and keep my phone disconnected out of business hours, I'm sure the culprit will give up in the end.'

'If I were your husband for real I'd insist on notifying the police.'

'Possibly. But don't even think of trying it, Sinclair.'

'I won't. But only because I know how you react when people try to run your life. Don't work too hard, Rose. See you later.'

Rose dressed at top speed, ate some breakfast, and before she opened up hurried along the arcade to do some shopping for her unexpected dinner party, wondering if she'd lost her mind as she selected a meal likely to please her guest. She knew very well she should be wary of the underlying resentment James so very obviously harboured along with the desire he still felt for her, but in some ways it just added an extra spice of danger to the pleasure of seeing him again. Much as she loved Chastlecombe, life there tended to be on the quiet side. And right now the sun was shining, a touch of spring was in the air, and, whatever happened afterwards, tonight she would enjoy spending time with James just once more. Because, quite apart from reviving old hurts, meeting him again had reminded her of a very important aspect of her relationship with James Sinclair. As well as being crazy about each other, for a few short, sweet months they'd been best friends as well as lovers. A combination that had made James such a hard act to follow.

Rose stowed her shopping away, then went to collect the post and start the day.

'Goodness me,' said Bel soon afterwards. 'You look very bouncy today, boss. What's put the sparkle in *your* eye?'

'Promise of spring in the air.'

'Wish it would do the same for me. Seeing Anthony tonight?'

'No, not tonight.' Rose hesitated, then decided on the truth. 'I've invited an old college friend to dinner,' she said, smiling.

'An old *male* college friend, I trust?'

'Absolutely.'

'Close friend?'

'Used to be.'

'Brilliant!' said Bel, who disapproved of Anthony Garrett. 'Have fun.'

The day was busy, as most Saturdays were, and the morning passed so quickly Rose was remorseful when Bel had to beg off for lunch and shopping.

'Sorry, sorry. I didn't realise it was so late. Bring a sandwich back for me. Something extravagant.'

While Bel was away Rose's heart sank as she saw Anthony come in. He gave her a brooding look, then turned his back to browse round the shelves while she was busy with customers, but the moment the shop was empty he pounced on her belligerently.

'Where the blazes were you last night, Rose? I rang several times.'

'I know. I got your messages.'

'I asked you to ring back.'

'It was too late when I got home—'

'Where from?'

'I don't have to give you details of my movements, Anthony,' she said curtly, then looked up with a smile of relief as Bel came rushing back.

'Sorry I took so long,' Bel said breathlessly, handing over a paper sack. 'Crab salad, and it's fab. Hello, Anthony,' she added, offhand.

'Bel.' He nodded distantly. 'A word in private, Rose, if you would.'

She nodded, resigned. 'Come in the office, then, while I eat my lunch.'

'Can't we go up to the flat?' he complained, as he closed the door behind him.

'Not on a Saturday. Bel could be inundated any minute.' Rose took an appreciative bite of her sandwich. 'Talk away,' she said indistinctly.

'You know why I'm here,' he began, very obviously irritated by her attitude.

Rose shook her head. 'Actually, I don't.'

'Of course you do. To change your mind about tonight.'

'Sorry. No can do.'

His lips thinned. 'You're just being childish, Rose.'

She shook her head at him reprovingly. 'Your powers of persuasion need work, Anthony. Besides, I'm doing something else tonight.'

'But when I'm here you spend Saturdays with me!'

'Not every Saturday, and certainly not tonight.' Rose looked at him squarely. 'In fact, not any more. I'm afraid it's over between us, Anthony.'

He stared at her incredulously. '*Over?* What are you talking about? Only a short while ago we were discussing marriage—'

'No, Anthony. That was your idea, not mine.'

'Oh, I get it!' His face suffused with angry colour. 'Sinclair's to blame for all this, isn't he? You're still in love with him.'

'No,' said Rose curtly. 'That's nothing to do with it. You and I just wouldn't suit on a long-term basis, Anthony, so it's best to end things now before either of us gets hurt.' She held out her hand. 'Can we at least part friends?'

He gave her a look of burning dislike, brushed the hand aside and wrenched open the door, forcing a smile when he spotted someone he knew amongst the people browsing along Rose's shelves.

'I've been dying to ask all afternoon, but we've been too busy,' said Bel, as she was getting ready to leave for the day. 'By the look on Anthony's face earlier I assume all is at an end?'

Rose heaved a sigh. 'Afraid so.'

'Can't say I'm sorry.' Bel gave her a swift, unaccustomed kiss on her cheek. 'Have some real fun instead with your friend. And tell me all about it on Monday.'

After Rose locked up the shop she did some swift housework, had a shower, did more to her hair with a styling brush than usual, then dithered about for a while in front of her open wardrobe. Nothing too special, she warned herself, and buttoned a thin, blush-pink cardigan to its plunging V-neck, pulled on navy linen drawstring trousers she'd been keeping for the summer, then wrapped herself in a striped apron, and repaired to the kitchen to get to work.

Potatoes were scrubbed, hollandaise sauce prepared for the asparagus, and monkfish tails wrapped in bacon ready to roast by the time Rose laid a small table under a window which in daylight gave a view of rolling Cotswold hills. And realised she was in a state of excitement unknown since she was eighteen years old. When she'd been so young and vulnerable, and so hopelessly in love with James Sinclair. But all that was changed, she assured herself, as eight o'clock loomed nearer. Tonight she would discuss the forthcoming separation sensibly with James, and after that they could go their separate ways. Because spending time with a man who made it gratifying plain he both resented and desired her was asking for trouble, when the man in question was the husband she was still married to.

When the bell rang at last Rose went sedately down the stairs, unable to control her body's leap of response when she found James standing there, arms full of bottles, his eyes bright with sudden heat at the sight of her.

Warning bells in Rose's head. He was reading too much into her invitation to dinner. 'Hello, James,' she said, smiling politely. 'You're punctual.'

'I'd have been earlier if I'd thought you'd let me in,' he assured her, and closed the door behind them, slamming the bolts home with a finality far too symbolic for Rose's peace of mind. 'I brought some wine. If you want the red I need to open it for breathing space. Or you can chill the white instead.' He smiled down at her. 'Or we could drink both.'

Rose retreated up the stairs hurriedly, conscious that his eyes were on her rear view as she went.

'I already have some wine. But thanks, anyway. I'll keep yours for another time.' She waved him to the sofa. 'Dinner will be half an hour, so we could start on my wine now, if you like. Or I've got whisky, gin—'

'Rose,' he interrupted, and dumped the bottle down to take her hands. 'You're as jumpy as a cat.'

'Yes, I am,' she said bluntly. 'I think this may be a mistake.'

'You're worried I might try to get you into bed before dinner, or after?' he said affably.

Rose stared up into teasing eyes, then relaxed, and laughed. 'Something like that.' she admitted.

'Is that how Garrett behaves?' he demanded.

'Not with me.' She picked up the wine and went to the kitchen, then turned in the doorway to look at James over her shoulder. 'Which doesn't mean I've led a totally celibate life from the time you and I split up, Sinclair.'

'Likewise,' said James promptly. 'But I knew very well you and Garrett weren't lovers.'

'How?'

'Something in the body language.' He shook his head. 'He's not the man for you, Rose.'

'I'll get the wine,' she said firmly, and went to oversee her dinner preparations.

The meal was a success, and James sincere with his praise as he despatched his dinner with gratifying speed.

'That was fabulous. You're a great cook, Rose,' he said, sitting back at last.

She shook her head. 'Just a fan of TV cooking programmes. You were a guinea pig tonight. I've never tried monkfish before.'

'It was superb,' James assured her, and refilled their wine glasses. His eyes were intent as he leaned back in his chair. 'You know, Rose, I used to think about this a lot. Meeting you again, sharing a meal like this—just being together.'

Rose eyed him cynically as she got up to take their plates. 'In which case you could have done something about it long before now if you'd wanted to. I wasn't exactly on another planet.'

'I was a coward,' he said flatly, and followed her to the kitchen.

'A *coward*? You, James?'

'I couldn't face more rejection.'

She gave him a scornful, disbelieving look as she handed him a platter of cheese and biscuits. 'You take these; I'll bring celery and grapes. No pudding. I did consider treacle tart from the bakery, then I remembered you weren't keen on sweet things in the past.'

'Only on you, Rose,' he agreed, standing aside to let her pass.

'"Sweet" wasn't one of the adjectives you flung at me during our final encounter all those years ago,' she reminded him acidly. 'So if you had come to see me again some time I suppose you're right. I might well have shut the door in your face.'

'After I saw you in the street with this Mark of yours I worked that out for myself.' James put the plates on the table, then took her hand. 'Could we eat this later?'

'OK. Coffee?'

'No. Come and sit down.' James led her to the sofa and drew her down beside him. 'Did you soften towards me after you left university?'

'I was in London by then, learning to earn a living, and far too busy to mourn for you.' She gave him a sidelong glance through her lashes. 'I admit I used to imagine, sometimes, that I spotted you in the street. But it was always just some tall, dark stranger with a king-of-the-jungle walk like yours.'

James kept hold of her hand, his forefinger smoothing the back of it. 'So you're certain you'd have rejected me second time round, Rose.'

'Definitely.' Her eyes hardened. 'Like you, I rarely make the same mistake twice.'

James tensed, and for a moment she thought he was going to leap to his feet and stride out of the flat. Instead he raised her hand to his lips. 'I'm sure I could change your mind about that,' he said, in a tone that sent trickles of apprehension down her spine.

'I don't think so,' she said doggedly, and got to her feet, holding onto her resolve with both hands. 'I think it's time you went, James.'

He got up with the lithe grace she remembered so well, looking like a tiger balked of its prey. 'What if I don't want to go, Rose?' And before she could dodge away he pulled her up into his arms, kissing her with an abruptness that excited her so much she responded involuntarily, all her cool resolutions flying through the window at the first touch of his lips, her hands making only nominal resistance as he began to slide buttons from their moorings.

'You can't *do* this,' she gasped, trying to push him away. 'Do you really think you can march back into my life after ten years and straight into my bed?'

'Who said anything about bed?' he said, frustrating her attempts to free herself. 'What's the harm in a few kisses, Rose Sinclair?'

'Don't call me that,' she snapped, twisting in his arms, but he held her fast.

'It's your name. And I'm still your husband.'

'Only technically—' But the rest of her words were smothered as James began to kiss her again, making love to her with a subtlety that broke down all the barriers she'd tried so hard to erect against him. Her mouth parted helplessly to his demanding tongue, and she sucked in her breath as he caught her flailing hands in one of his and bared her breasts to his lips and teeth and relentless, clever fingers, rousing hot, wet turbulence deep inside her as he bore her further down on the sofa, his breath coming in great gasps as he raised his head to look down into her flushed, desire-blank face.

'You still want me, admit it,' James said hoarsely, the breath rasping through his chest, triumph in his voice bringing Rose back to earth with a bump.

She shoved him away in disgust, and jumped to her feet, desire transformed to blazing anger. 'Is that what all this is about?' she threw at him. 'An ego-massaging exercise?' She let out a strangled sound of self-loathing as she put herself back together with shaking fingers, then shoved him away as he tried to take her in his arms.

'Rose,' he panted, capturing her hands. 'Don't look at me like that.'

She calmed down a little. 'It was my fault,' she said bitterly. 'I should never have asked you round here tonight.' She blinked away angry tears. 'Like a stupid idiot I thought we could just talk rationally, like adult human beings. Whereas you took it for granted I had a spot of auld lang syne in mind.'

James released her and stood back. 'I'm only human, Rose. And male. I needed to know if you still responded to me.'

'Well, now you do,' she said wearily. 'You've made the experiment and it worked like a charm. I hope your wilting ego is satisfied.'

He gave her a deeply disturbing smile. 'Bad choice of words, Rose. But if I promise not to come within a foot of you until I leave could we still have that rational talk? And maybe the coffee we passed on earlier?'

Rose stared at him, irresolute, then gave a deep, shaky sigh. 'All right,' she said dully. 'Why not? We can discuss the divorce.'

'What if I said I don't want a divorce?' he parried.

She swallowed, thrusting a hand through her tumbled hair. 'Don't start that again. Because whether you do or not, James, is immaterial. I can get one any time I want.'

His smile set her teeth on edge. 'In that case, Rose, tell me what made you wait all these years before doing something about it?'

Good question, thought Rose, later that night, while sleep became less and less of a possibility as the hours dragged by. The coffee had been a mistake, since James had flatly refused to discuss the divorce, and in the end had taken his leave without kissing her again, but with a faintly ominous promise to be in touch.

And what, exactly, did he mean by that? thought Rose, pummelling her pillow yet again. Tonight was meant to be a full stop. A finale to the unfinished business between them.

After a Sunday spent alone and restless, hoping James would contact her again, halfway through Monday Rose discovered exactly what James had meant by keeping in touch when the local florist delivered a vast sheaf of spring flowers.

'Thank you for a delightful evening. J.S.,' was the message.

'I assume J.S. is the old chum,' said Bel, eyes dancing, '*Very* nice. You obviously had a good time together.'

Rose smiled in agreement, and took the flowers up to her flat, glad that the rest of the day was busy enough to keep her mind off James Sinclair. But later that evening the phone rang while she was deep in publishers' catalogues, checking on titles in the pipeline.

With the caution she'd acquired lately she waited until she heard James begin to leave a message before she picked up the receiver.

'How are you today, Rose?'

'Tired. We've been busy. I lost your phone number,' she fibbed, 'so I had no way of thanking you for the flowers.'

'Just a small token of appreciation. And for obvious reasons, not roses. It occurred to me that you don't have my home address. So grab a pen.' He gave her his home and mobile number, and his London address. 'Try not to lose them this time. Though in emergencies you can always reach me at the bank.'

'I doubt I'll need to do that! Future communications,' added Rose crisply, 'will probably be made through my solicitor.'

James laughed mockingly. 'You really believe that? Goodnight, Rose.'

Rose was very much aware that this was the day she should have instructed Henry to start proceedings, but she hadn't been able to bring herself to do it. Because in her heart of hearts she didn't want to be free of James. At least, not yet. Her intellect resented his assumption that he could just invade her life again and sweep her off her feet to show he still had power over her. But her errant heart, not to mention the body that throbbed at the mere sound of his voice, made it plain that only sheer force of will had helped her hold out against him. The sensible course would be to break all contact with him once and for all, and be safe. But then, when had she ever been sensible in her dealings with James Sinclair?

And James, she discovered, had no intention of letting her break contact. He phoned every night, ostensibly to check on her stalker, then to chat for a while, and if the intention was to keep Rose in a state of suspense every night until he called James was highly successful. She found it hard to settle to anything until she'd heard from him, and even refused Bel's invitation to a meal at the weekend in favour of staying in for the nightly conversation with James.

'I'm in bed, James,' she snapped, one night towards the end of the week, irritable because she'd been waiting on tenterhooks for what seemed like hours.

'If I woke you up it's your fault. Your line was engaged early on, before I went out. I've only just got back. Who were you talking to, anyway?'

'Let me see.' Rose relaxed, smiling smugly at the ceiling. 'Mark Cummings, Henry Beresford, oh, and Anthony Garrett.'

There was a tense pause. 'I don't know which one I object to most,' said James tightly. 'But on consideration perhaps it's Henry Beresford. Was the subject divorce, by any chance?'

She stretched luxuriously, deeply gratified by his tone. 'Yes.'

Another silence. 'And Garrett? What did he want?'

'In a word, me. He decided to overlook my aberration last weekend, and proposed marriage again.'

'Remind the bastard that you're not a free agent,' said James savagely. 'So what did Cummings want?'

'To talk about the bookstall I'm running at his school tomorrow night.'

'As long as that's all he wants.'

'My personal life is nothing to do with you any more, Sinclair.'

He laughed softly, with a mocking indulgence that clenched her fists. 'Goodnight. Sweet dreams. I'll call you.'

CHAPTER ELEVEN

ROSE went off with her wares to run the stall at Chastlecombe Grammar School parents' evening without hearing from James. Disappointed, and furious with herself because of it, she got through the evening with her usual smiling efficiency, accepted Mark's help in clearing up, and his company on the way home to help her take everything into the shop. Refusing her offer of coffee, Mark gave her a hug and a kiss on the front doorstep, told her to lock up securely behind him and went sprinting home to his little daughter.

Rose dawdled over her preparations for bed, but the longed-for phone call refused to materialise. She lay awake for hours, but heard nothing from James until he strolled into the shop next morning in person. Rose, bowled over at the sight of him, was involved with a customer, but Bel, in tune at once to the gamma rays sizzling between her boss and the newcomer, gave James a beaming welcome and volunteered her help in supplying him with the latest additions to their non-fiction section.

The moment the shop was empty Rose made the necessary introductions, and tactful Bel promptly took herself off to a very early lunch hour.

'You didn't say you were coming down again, James,' said Rose, eyeing him with resentment.

'If I had you'd probably have taken off somewhere else,' said James, and leaned against the counter to look into her eyes. 'We need to talk.'

Rose clenched her teeth against the wave of pure longing that swept through her, and saw James's eyes dilate as he sensed it. 'We can't talk here,' she whispered, as a trio of customers entered the shop.

'Tonight, then.'

'No. I'm going out to dinner—'

'No, you're not. Cancel!' His eyes took on a steely gleam. 'Do it, Rose. I'll be round later.' He picked up his book and strode from the shop, leaving her in a state of such tension she was glad the newcomers were content to browse for a while before requiring her attention.

'That was the old college chum, I assume,' said Bel, when she came back.

Rose nodded. 'I wasn't expecting him.'

'I could see that. I thought I'd have to scrape you up from the floor.' Bel grinned. 'You're a dark horse, Rose Dryden. No wonder you passed on my offer tonight!'

It was the longest Saturday Rose had ever experienced. By the time she closed the shop she was tense with a variety of emotions ranging from plain weariness to a state of euphoria that made her feel sick. She went through the motions of locking up and leaving everything secure for the night, then trudged upstairs, wondering how soon James was likely to turn up. This time she had no special meal in readiness. If he wanted food James would have to provide it. And probably cook it too, in her present state of exhaustion.

Rose stood under the shower for a long time, dried her hair, dressed in the navy linen trousers and a white cotton sweater, added a few basic touches to her face, and made herself some tea. She curled up on her sofa with it, but before she'd taken more than a sip or two her phone rang. She snatched up the receiver eagerly, expecting James, then shuddered as she heard her name whispered before the line went dead. She slammed the phone down, not even bothering to try and trace the call as she cursed the idiot who was frightening her. When the doorbell rang she raced down the stairs, then gave a gasp of horror as she stumbled over a newly delivered rose in her headlong flight. She flung the door open, tears streaming down her face, and James stared at slammed the door shut behind him.

'My God, Rose, what's wrong—?' He stopped short as she held out the flower, and with a savage curse he flung it down and took her in his arms, holding her close, murmuring wordless comfort into her hair as she sobbed her heart out against his chest. After a minute or two James picked her up and carried her up to the flat, and sat down with her in his lap, smoothing her head against his shoulder as he let her cry.

'Better now?' he whispered, when she was quiet at last.

'Yes,' said Rose thickly, and sat up, knuckling the tears from her eyes. 'Sorry to make such a fuss. It was a hard day, I'd just had another of those phone calls, and the flower was the final straw. I just hate this feeling of being watched.' She looked up into his eyes, trying to smile. 'I must look a mess,' she added, pushing her hair back.

'No, you don't.' James drew her down against his shoulder again. 'You look delectable.' He narrowed his eyes at her. 'Nor, I discovered last night, am I the only one who thinks so.'

Rose frowned. 'What do you mean?'

'I came round to see you last night the minute I arrived, and saw you in a clinch with another man.' His jaw clenched. 'I assume the guy kissing you was Mark Cummings?'

'Oh. Yes. He helped me home with my stock,' she said,

secretly euphoric. 'Why didn't you say something? I waited hours—' She stopped dead.

'What for?' he asked, so silkily she tried to pull away, but his arms tightened. 'Were you waiting for me to ring, by any chance? If I had I'd have blown my top, lady, after watching you kiss another man.'

'It was just a goodnight peck,' said Rose truculently. 'Mark's an old friend.'

'Which doesn't give him the right to make love to my wife.'

'I'm not—'

'Oh, yes, you are. I'm still your husband and you're still my wife, Rose Sinclair. I've got every right to make love to you,' he whispered, raising the hairs along her spine. 'And I want you. Now.'

Their eyes met. Rose could feel his arousal hard beneath her thighs, and her heart began to beat thickly, every nerve-ending heightened by recent fright, and present longing, and a deep, uncontrollable need to feel James's body joined with hers in the rapture she had never come near to experiencing with anyone else. Even if tonight was all she'd have, she wanted it. And wanted it badly. She shivered uncontrollably as James, eyes blazing with triumph, took her silence for assent.

He kissed her as though he was starved for her, and Rose surrendered to him with equal hunger, responding wantonly as their lips and tongues and importuning hands synchronised in a love duet which quickly threatened to reach crescendo.

'Wait,' gasped Rose.

'I *can't* wait!' James pushed her flat beneath him and smothered her protests with kisses that drove everything from her mind as their mutual need roared through them like a forest fire, consuming them so rapidly they clutched each other close. As they shockwaves receded afterwards, their eyes locked in mutual awe.

Without a word James picked her up and carried her to the bedroom, where he relieved her to the remainder of her clothes at dizzying speed, then demanded a similar service in return.

'No,' gasped Rose, trembling under the eyes which caressed her body with tactile hunger. 'You do it. I'll be too slow.'

'I thought you'd lived with someone!'

'I didn't do that kind of thing for him.'

'Why not?' he whispered, stretching out beside her.

'I just couldn't,' she said impatiently, and lay with eyes closed for a moment to savour the bliss of head-to-toe contact again as he smoothed her body against his. The first time, James had removed only enough clothing to make their loving possible. But now they were together in full naked contact their bodies generated a heat that quickly rekindled their mutual fire.

'I've got a lot of time to make up for,' whispered James, his breath hot against her ear. 'And this time I mean to go slow, so pay attention.'

He began to make love to her in the way she'd so often dreamed of and longed for, his lips pulling on taut, hard nipples as his probing fingers caressed and cajoled. Soon she was one aching, shivering mass of hot, liquid longing as he deliberately inflamed them both to such unbearable heights of arousal he gasped her name at last and entered her with a sure, conquering thrust and united them again, as they were always meant to be, in one flesh.

Rose's breath was still tearing through her chest as James turned her face up to his afterwards, his eyes hot on hers. 'Now tell me you're not in love with me any more!'

She stiffened in his arms. 'Is that what all this is about? To make me admit I still find you irresistible, Sinclair?'

'Not entirely. I know your body responds to me, Rose.' He smiled a little. 'I tried to convince myself that I'd fantasised about what we had together. That it couldn't possibly have been as good as I remembered. And it isn't.'

She glared at him, and he laughed and kissed her heard. 'It's even better.' He sobered abruptly. 'But it was never just physical for us, Rose. I need to know you still care.'

Rose gazed up into his eyes for a long time, unwilling to commit herself, then threw caution to the winds. Of course she cared. So what was the point in pretending she didn't? 'Yes,' she said gruffly. 'I care.'

His engulfing kiss put an end to conversation for a while, until her stomach gave an unromantic grumble and James laughed indulgently.

'You're hungry. What can I do about it?'

Rose sat up, pulling the covers up to hide her breasts from grey, marauding eyes. 'One,' she said, ticking off her fingers, 'you can order in something from Orsini's and wait for hours until we eat, two, you could go out and buy fish and chips, or three, we can eat bacon and eggs right now.'

'Three,' said James promptly. 'I'm starving.'

A few minutes later, fully dressed and more or less in her right mind, Rose had bacon, eggs and mushrooms ready, accompanied by hunks of bread. They sat together on the sofa, and for a while James ate in famished, appreciative silence. But once the meal was over he looked at her with searching eyes.

'So what happens now, Rose?' He took her hand. 'Come and sit on my lap and let's discuss it.'

When they were settled together in familiar embrace,

with Rose's head on James's shoulder, he put a finger under her chin and turned her face up to his.

'Does this mean you've changed your mind about the divorce?'

Rose met his eyes steadily. 'Do you want me to?'

'What else did you think all that was about?' he demanded, then frowned. 'However, like the late, unlamented Mr Garrett, I'm based in London. Will this be a problem?'

'No, it won't,' she said emphatically. 'Because I'm not rushing into anything this time, James.'

He eyed her askance. 'I don't like the sound of that. Hell, Rose, we've wasted too much time apart already.'

'Nevertheless, I'm not a starry-eyed teenager any more, James. I've acquired at least *some* common sense since I saw you last.'

He kissed the lip she was biting. 'To hell with common sense. It's time you made up for all the years you forced us to spend apart.'

Rose drew in a deep, unsteady breath. 'James, we need to get to know each other again before I do that.'

'Why? Surely we've both matured into responsible adults.'

She touched a hand to his cheek. 'No one could have acted more responsibly than you did ten years ago, James, when I came crying to you with my little problem.'

His eyes darkened. 'It was no big deal, Rose. I knew you had no parents to turn to. It never occurred to me to do anything other than assume full responsibility.'

'And I was desperately grateful for that. But so guilty, too, about your finals.' She smiled a little. 'You were well-known for concentrating on books rather than girls.'

'Until I met you.' He kissed her again. 'And, just in case you're wondering, there's no significant female presence in my life, I promise.' He smiled crookedly. 'Though I confess to acquaintance with more than one lady not averse to the odd spot of wining, dining and bed, now and then.'

'Lord, you're arrogant!'

'Just truthful. I'm a normal male animal and own up to certain needs from time to time.' He smoothed her hair back from her forehead. 'If I had you all that would be over, I promise.'

'But living with someone can be tricky,' said Rose, resisting the urge to say yes to everything he asked.

'We managed it very happily during the brief times we managed to spend together,' he reminded her.

'Maybe because we never had enough of it—time, I mean,' she added, flushing.

'So let's make up for it now,' said James, his eyes locked with hers as he stroked a finger along the hectic colour in her cheek.

'Not so fast,' she said breathlessly. 'I think we should work up to it gradually, just seeing each other socially for a while. Going out to dinner—'

'Out?' he mocked. 'Did you actually say *out* to dinner?'

'I did.'

'Hallelujah!' James paused, eyeing her narrowly. 'Or did you mean in London where no one knows us?'

'Right here in Chastlecombe, too.' Rose smiled at him cajolingly. 'What do you say?'

'In what capacity am I to do this as far as this town is concerned?' enquired James. 'Officially as your husband, or just as a replacement for Mr Garrett?'

'I'll have to think about that,' she said, frowning. 'If this is to be a sort of testing period, to find out if marriage is a practical proposition for us—'

'Rose,' he said impatiently, 'We *are* married!'

'Only on paper.' She looked at him in appeal. 'But before I burn my boats I need you to be very sure about this, James. I don't mean what happened between us just now,' she added, colouring. 'In that way we're still totally compatible—'

'Agreed. So what's the problem?' he demanded.

'A very prosaic one.' Rose sighed. 'My only attempt at actually living with a man was a total disaster.'

'With me it will be different, I promise,' he said with supreme confidence, and kissed her as emphasis. He drew back to look down into her eyes. 'So tell me you're willing to take the chance, Rose.'

She looked at him in silence for a moment, then nodded slowly. 'Yes. I am.'

His eyes lit with satisfaction. 'But if I come courting for all your world to see, I need assurances. My ego couldn't take another hammering from you, Rose.'

'It won't have to.' She looked at him in sudden disbelief. 'James, we're going too fast—'

'Not fast enough for me!'

It was very late by the time Rose made a pot of coffee to drink with cheese and biscuits. 'A recipe for insomnia if ever I saw one,' she commented.

James smiled slowly. 'I know an infallible cure for that—or would you rather I slept at the cottage tonight?'

'When are you going back to London?'

'Tomorrow evening. After I've spent as much of Sunday as possible with you.'

Rose looked at him for a moment. 'Not much point in going back to the cottage, then. Stay the night.'

James reached for her and pulled her close, a look in his eyes that sent a cold shiver down her spine.

'What is it?' she whispered.

'I'm thinking of all the time wasted,' he said bitterly,

and held her face cupped in his hands. 'You owe me, Rose.'

After Rose had paid some of the debt to James's satisfaction they fell asleep in each other's arms, and woke to make love again in the early morning before the world outside was awake.

'Do you still have your wedding ring?' said James later, over the breakfast they'd brought back to bed to eat.

'Of course I have.' She frowned as she considered her hand. 'I was never able to wear it back then, so maybe it won't even fit me now.'

'If it doesn't I'll buy you another one,' he said promptly, but Rose shook her head.

'I want that one. It can be altered if it doesn't fit.'

'So when will you start wearing it again?'

'When we go public, I suppose. Which had better be soon, now Anthony knows about you. Minerva will be surprised. Henry's expecting to arrange a divorce.' Rose looked at him questioningly. 'How about you? Will you tell your mother?'

'Yes, but not over the phone. I'll go up to see her.' James leaned over to kiss a smear of marmalade from Rose's cheek. 'Messy eater,' he said indulgently.

'It's so difficult in bed,' she said, laughing. 'Look out, mind your coffee!'

'I vote we eat lunch elsewhere.' He brushed toast crumbs away. 'Sorry—you'll have to change your bed before you sleep in it again.'

'Pity,' said Rose with regret, and gave him a sparkling look. 'I was hoping to keep your smell to sleep with tonight.'

'My smell!'

'Scent, then.' She leaned nearer to nuzzle his shoulder, sucking delicately at his skin. 'I'd know yours anywhere.'

James gave a strangled sound, slid out of bed, removed the breakfast tray, then got back in and took Rose in his arms all in one movement. 'I'd know you anywhere, too, Rose Sinclair,' he whispered against her mouth. 'So, if you were intending to read the Sunday papers at this point, you're out of luck.'

CHAPTER TWELVE

WHEN James left her, far later that evening than he'd intended, Rose had time at last to think. Too much time. She felt restless, and roamed the flat like a lost soul, switching on the television, switching it off again, trying to read the Sunday papers neither of them had looked at. When her cellphone rang at last Rose felt limp with relief when she heard the voice she'd been waiting for.

'What have you been doing since I left?' he asked.

'Nothing much. I'm a bit tired.'

'Lack of sleep last night,' he said, audibly smug.

'Yes.' Rose heaved a sigh. 'I don't foresee sleeping all that well tonight, either.'

'Because you're head over heels in love with me?' he said swiftly.

'Something like that.'

'Good,' he said triumphantly. 'I'll remind you of that next time we meet. Talking of which,' he said after a pause, 'that won't be for a while. I'm afraid I'm off to Boston for the job on Thursday. I'll be up the following weekend.'

A whole fortnight. Which would be for the best, in some ways. 'In that case, James,' she said slowly, 'could I come down to you that weekend? If I am going to move in with you I'd like to see where you live.'

There was silence for a moment. 'Rose, could we postpone that for a while?'

'Of course,' she said instantly, rebuffed.

He swore softly. 'You're offended.'

'Not in the least. I'll come some other time. Or not, according to how things go.'

'Stop that right now, Rose! Come by all means. I just wanted the house to look less of a mess before you did. Until very recently I shared it with someone else.'

Who? thought Rose, picturing some voluptuous female making off in a huff with designer luggage. 'It's all right,' she said carelessly. 'It was just an idea. Let's leave it awhile.'

James let out an exasperated sigh. 'I shall expect you here a week on Saturday evening, Rose, so arrange it.'

Mondays in the shop were usually busy, and Rose was glad of it after the emotional ups and downs of her weekend. She had slept badly for more than one reason after the unexpected little tiff with James, and felt on edge until he rang that evening.

'I've rung to apologise,' he said without preamble.

'What about?'

'For not welcoming your visit with open arms.'

'It was certainly a bit off-putting after I'd—'

'Made mad, passionate love with me for most of the weekend?'

'Beautifully put,' she said acidly. 'Look, James, I don't have to come.'

'Don't dare back out now, Rose. I've organised a cleaning company to come in next week to make the place habitable. Just for you. It's going to be a hell of a long fortnight, so what time do I expect you? Early as possible, please.'

'Actually,' said Rose carefully, 'I could make it on the Friday evening. If you like.'

'Damn right I like!' He paused. 'Hopefully the cleaners should be finished by then, but I'll probably be working late with the risk management boys, so I'll send you a key. You can let yourself in if you're before me. And explore Bluebeard's lair to your heart's content,' he added slyly. 'Who's minding the store for you?'

'Minerva's volunteered. She likes to keep a finger on the pulse occasionally, anyway. I think she misses contact with the general public.'

'Will you miss that, too?'

'Probably.'

'Enough for second thoughts?' he demanded.

'No.'

'Then tell me again you're still mad about me.'

'How many times do I have to say it to convince you?'

'A lot more yet, lady.'

'I'll tell you—no, I'll *show* you when I see you.'

The time dragged by while James was away, with only his phone calls to reassure Rose she hadn't dreamed the passionate weekend in his arms. By the time her train arrived at Ealing Broadway just under a fortnight later she was in such a state of tension her head was aching as she took a taxi to a house in one of the suburb's broad, leafy roads. Feeling rather furtive, she let herself into James's empty home, put her bag down in the square hall, then went exploring the large, conventional house. The sitting room was big, with rugs scattered here and there on polished wood floors, chairs and sofas covered in new-looking sand-coloured linen, paler curtains looped and swagged round a large bay window. Books filled the shelves in alcoves flanking a fireplace topped by a glowing oil of a Highland loch at sunset.

Rose looked round her with a sudden, fierce sense of possession. She liked it here. She wanted to live here. Whoever had lived here before.

After a moment's hesitation she went upstairs to look

into James's bedroom, which was spartan and very tidy. She looked at the wide bed, then wished she hadn't as a hot rush of excitement intensified the throbbing in her head. Wondering if James was ever in need of a painkiller she had a look in his bathroom with no result, then went back along the landing to the main bathroom. In a cabinet which held a sparse selection of male toiletries, she found a few basic medical supplies, and a box of tampons and a half-empty bottle of expensive French perfume. Rose clenched her teeth against a sudden rush of nausea. James had been frank about other women, but it was a shock to come face to face with such personal confirmation of his past. Did these things belong to the former tenant, or merely one of the women happy to share bed and board with James on a casual basis?

It has been ten years, she reminded herself stringently. What did you expect? She swallowed down a couple of painkillers with a glass of water, then went back into the master bedroom to examine the leather folder on James's dresser. It held two snapshots: one was of a lurcher, with a schoolboy James embracing it as he grinned at the camera, the other showed two people flanking young James with fishing rod, the woman's face obscured by a cotton sun hat, the tired man gazing down on his son with such deep affection Rose felt a lump in her throat. A third, unframed photograph lay face down on the chest. Rose turned it over, and eyed it with deep hostility. A young blonde woman of her own age, with expensively cut hair and a black dress which clung to every curve, lounged, laughing, on what looked like the sofa downstairs. The eyes held a smile of such confident, teasing allure Rose's fingers curled, wanting to tear the photograph in shreds.

Rose heard the door slam downstairs, and put the photograph down guiltily. She ran downstairs, and without a word James dumped down his briefcase and swept her into his arms, kissing her with a hunger she responded to involuntarily, unable to control her body's reaction to his touch after so long.

'God, it's been a long time,' he said at last, rubbing his cheek over her hair. 'I wondered if you'd be here, after all.'

Rose stood back to look up at him. 'I very nearly wasn't. Your initial lack of enthusiasm was very off-putting,' she said frankly. 'I almost told you to get lost again then and there.'

'I could tell that,' said James, grimacing. 'So I re-grouped in a hurry. Come here. I've been thinking about this for two long weeks, woman.'

'So have I.' Pushing the photograph from her mind, Rose returned the kiss with such fervour James thrust her away at last, his breathing ragged.

'Let me take you on a tour,' he said gruffly. 'Otherwise I'm likely to carry you straight up to bed right now. And then you might think I'm only after your body.'

'You want more than that?'

'Damn right. I want every last thing you have to offer, Rose Sinclair,' said James, and shrugged off his long dark overcoat. 'How much have you seen?'

'Only your sitting room and some of the upstairs.' Which last had been a bit of a mistake. She smiled as they went into his sitting room. 'You must have found my place a bit claustrophobic after this.'

'You were there, Rose. I didn't notice much else.' He looked around him. 'The cleaning people seem to have done a good job. They've put the new covers on for me, I see. Alex left me a couple of chairs, so with a bit of input from my mother I had them married up with the same material.' His eyes returned to Rose, bright with something she thought she identified as decision. 'But if you don't like anything I'll change it—in fact if you don't like the house we'll find somewhere else.'

'I love it here.' Rose reached up and kissed him, forcing herself to keep quiet about the woman in the photograph.

'Then come and see the rest of it.'

James took her on a tour of an empty dining room and a study at the back, which shared a view of the garden with a kitchen some former owner had been clever enough to enlarge and modernise without losing its character.

'When I bought the place Alex came in with me as my tenant, which helped with the mortgage. I lived downstairs, Alex up here,' he said, preceding her upstairs. 'But now the master bedroom's all mine.' James paused beside the large bed, his eyes intent on her face. 'Rose,' he said huskily, reaching for her, 'don't make me wait any longer—'

'Not so fast,' said Rose. 'First tell me who this is.' She detached herself and picked up the photograph. 'Is she the reason you put me off coming, James? Was she still in residence at the time?'

He stared blankly at the photograph, then back at Rose, his eyes narrowed to a gleam which sent a chill down her spine. 'No, she was not. What kind of a man do you think I am?'

'After ten years how should I know?' she said, all the more militant because she'd expected him to reassure her. 'Is she one of the dinner-and-bed brigade? Or is *she* this Alex of yours?'

'Neither,' said James flatly, taking off his jacket.

'So why the secrecy?'

James's face set into cold implacable lines. 'I've had only one guilty secret in my life.' He smiled grimly. 'That was you. So if we're going to have any kind of viable relationship in future you need to take me on trust.'

'That's not fair!'

'Life isn't fair. I learned that early on at your hands, lady.'

Rose winced. 'Look, James, I came up here earlier. I had a headache and I was looking for painkillers. There's some perfume and—other things in your bathroom cabinet. Which made it obvious a woman's been in residence quite recently. Was that why you didn't want me to come?'

'No,' said James harshly. 'That wasn't the reason at all, but let's leave that for now.' He stalked across the room towards her, his eyes bright with such cold ferocity Rose had a sudden urge to turn and run. 'To set you right, my darling wife, no woman has ever lived here with me because I've never exposed myself to the dangers of a close relationship since the day I last saw you.'

Rose backed away, her headache suddenly excruciating. 'You haven't forgiven me at all have you, James?' she said unsteadily. 'So why in heaven's name did you have to make love to me if you felt like that? Punishment? Ego-boosting?'

'Before I saw you I didn't intend to make love to you at all,' he said bitterly. 'Once I did meet you, I was angry because I wanted you the minute I laid eyes on you again. So I hatched some crazy idea about turning the tables on you, making you fall in love with me. The way you'd done with me in the past.' He flung away to stare through the window.

Rose felt an icy chill seep through her as she stared at his back. 'That's why you kept on asking me to say I loved you,' she said dully. 'Why you never once returned the compliment. You just wanted revenge, didn't you,

James? All that talk about not wanting a divorce, living together, wedding rings, was just bait for the trap you set me.'

'*No*, it wasn't.' James turned sharply, and put out a hand in appeal, but Rose looked at it with such disdain he let it fall.

'If you'll call a cab I'll go home,' she said quietly.

His face hardened. 'Is that what you want?'

'It's not what I expected,' she said with a brittle smile, 'but under the circumstances it seems like a good idea.'

James shook his head. 'Look, we need to talk.'

'Too late for that,' she threw at him, and marched from the room, but he caught her back.

'Don't leave like this, Rose. Not now, when—'

'When what?' she said scornfully. 'You've had your fun with me, James Sinclair. Keep your wretched secrets. I wish you joy of them.'

'Oh, for God's sake,' he said in sudden fury. 'Alex is a hunk of Glaswegian testosterone by the name of Cargill. The woman in the photograph is his girlfriend. She was in and out of here all the time. The perfume must be hers.' He grabbed her by the shoulders. 'The cleaning people must have turned it up.'

Without warning Rose's headache suddenly reached crisis proportions, and with a gasped apology she fled into James's bathroom and parted with everything she'd eaten all day. When she emerged, ashen-faced and shivering, James put out a hand instinctively, then dropped it as she backed away.

'Sorry about that,' said Rose with what dignity she could muster.

'Would you like some tea?' he asked quietly.

'Thank you. I would.' She gave him a polite little smile. 'It's the travelling. I'm not good at it.'

'Go downstairs and curl up on a sofa while I change,' said James, suddenly all brisk sympathy. 'I'll make tea. Then we'll have that talk.'

'If we must,' said Rose listlessly, and drifted from the room, suddenly wanting to cry her eyes out at the way things had gone so contrary to the way she'd planned.

James came into the sitting room with a tray of tea, the investment banker metamorphosed into something more approachable in faded old sweatshirt and jeans. He poured tea into a beaker, added a splash of milk and handed it to her, then sat down beside her with his own. 'How do you feel?'

'Fragile,' said Rose, and drank some tea gingerly.

'Too fragile to listen?'

'I suppose not.'

'In that case let me explain in full.' James took the beaker from her and put it down on a table with his own. He took her hand in his. 'You remember your famous plan all those years ago, Rose?'

She gave him a derisive, sidelong glance. 'I'm hardly likely to forget, after the trouble it caused!'

'Right.' He frowned, looking down at their joined hands. 'I never forgot it, either. Nor you. Every time I met a woman I'd think I'd found the one to lay your ghost, Rose. But I never did. So when I received your letter I assured myself that I'd feel nothing for you after ten years. That you would be different. I'd be different. That we'd feel nothing for each other when we met again.'

He was wrong there, thought Rose.

'When we came face to face that night,' continued James, 'ten years disappeared like a flash of lightning, and the idea sprang fully-formed into my mind. Now it was your turn, I swore, before you'd even said a word. This time I'd be the one with the plan. I'd make you fall in love with me all over again, no matter how many men you had in your life.' He gave a short, derisive laugh. 'So much for ten years' maturity. What a fool!'

'Not really,' said Rose very quietly. 'Your plan was highly successful.'

James looked down at her. 'Was it? Truthfully, Rose?'

Her mouth twisted. 'Oh, yes. Ten years hadn't done much for my maturity either.'

He winced, his fingers tightening on hers. 'The reason I hesitated about having you here in my house was sheer, native Scots caution. I wanted to be utterly sure, first, that you were going to come back to me for good. Because *my* plan backfired. Whatever your feelings on the subject, I was the one who fell in love all over again.' He paused. 'So are you still going home, Rose?'

She hesitated. 'Actually, I don't feel very wonderful, so I think I will.'

James's mouth tightened. 'Walking out on me again?'

Rose looked at him hard and long. 'Look, I know you want me, James—'

'Dammit, Rose, I *love* you,' he said, and tried to take her in his arms, but she held him off.

'I believe that, too,' she said, surprised to find this was true. 'But you haven't forgiven me, James. Not really.'

'That's nonsense,' he said roughly.

'I don't think so...' Rose swallowed hard. 'Sorry, I feel sick again—'

He pulled her up and raced with her to a ground-floor cloakroom, and this time held her head as she threw up. Afterwards he washed her face gently, and smoothed her hair back, then, ignoring her protests, picked her up and carried her upstairs to his bed.

'Rest there for a while,' he said urgently. 'When you

feel up to it come downstairs and I'll concoct something tempting for your supper.'

Rose lay where she was for a long time, her arm over her eyes, her mind going round in circles. She got up gingerly at last, decided her stomach intended to behave, then washed her face and went downstairs to find him waiting in the hall.

'I heard you get up, Rose. You're very pale. What can I do for you?'

She ran her tongue round dry lips. 'Would you call a cab? I want to go home.'

'You can't travel like that,' he said impatiently.

'If I've got a stomach bug I'd rather cope with it at home.'

James thrust a hand through his hair in exasperation. 'I'd forgotten how stubborn you can be. All right, all right,' he added, as her mouth set mutinously. 'If you must go I'll drive you.'

The late Friday night traffic was heavy enough to prolong the journey, and by the time James drew up in the niche behind the shop Rose felt like death. Neither of them had said much in the car, but the things left unsaid had hung heavy in the air, and when James put her bag down in the sitting room Rose took her courage in both hands.

'I need to be on my own for a while, James.'

'Shouldn't you call a doctor?'

'Not tonight. If I'm not better in the morning I will.'

They looked at each other in silence.

'I don't want to part like this. What the hell went wrong, Rose?' demanded James.

'A stomach upset,' said Rose woodenly. 'An unromantic complaint. It needs privacy.'

James stiffened. 'Are you suggesting I turn tail and

drive back to London? Is that the kind of privacy you mean?'

'Yes. That's exactly what I mean.'

For a moment he stared at her in utter disbelief, then with a smothered exclamation he strode from the room and ran downstairs, banging the back door shut behind him.

Rose forced herself to go down and check that everything was secure, then she rang Minerva about the change of plan. 'But I'd like the day off tomorrow just the same,' she added apologetically. 'I feel terrible.'

James rang late that night after he arrived back in London. 'You and I have things to discuss.'

'I know,' said Rose wearily. 'But not right now. I need some time to myself.'

There was a pause. 'How much time?'

'A week or two?'

'If you need that much time away from me perhaps we should just pack it in altogether and go for the divorce,' he said savagely, and rang off.

When a couple of days went by with no word from James, Rose began to think he'd meant what he'd said.

'I just can't see why you told James to back off,' said Bel, who was now in possession of most of the facts. 'The minute I saw you both together it was obvious you were meant for each other.'

When she'd asked for time Rose hadn't expected James to take her quite so literally, and slept badly, the resulting shadows under her eyes causing comment when she joined Minerva and Henry for supper a day or two later. When Henry, with his usual tact, left them alone for a while after the meal Minerva eyed her niece searchingly.

'You look terrible, Rose. You're obviously pining for this James of yours. So what's wrong?'

'I have this rather ironic little problem,' said Rose bitterly. 'When I went to Cheltenham last week I bought a pregnancy test, and found a little blue line in the right— or the wrong—place.'

'Darling child!' Minerva got up and sat beside her, patting her hand. 'Are you sure?'

'That's the whole point,' said Rose miserably. 'James married me the first time round over a false alarm, so I waited until I'm absolutely certain this time.'

'Do you mind?' said her aunt gently.

'I don't mind about the baby, Minerva. But I mind because it complicates things. Last time James spoke to me he was angry with me, even made noises about getting on with the divorce. Though I don't think he meant that. I think—I *hope*—he was just angry because I pushed him away. I went down to London determined to tell him. But we had a row. And in the end I couldn't.' Her eyes filled. 'The baby's all my fault, anyway.'

'Not quite,' said Minerva dryly. 'James is at least half to blame.'

'But in the heat of the moment I never told him I don't take the necessary pills any more.' Rose blew her nose angrily. 'So now I'm pregnant, which is like holding a gun to his head.' She shuddered. 'I wanted us to be together because we can no longer bear to be apart, not because of James's sense of duty all over again.'

'Does he love you?'

'He says he does.'

'Do you love *him*.'

'Of course I love him,' said Rose tearfully, and jammed her knuckles in her eyes. 'Otherwise I wouldn't be in this stupid predicament.'

Rose was in bed, feeling very sorry for herself that night, when her cellphone rang.

'How are you, Rose?' said James, and she closed her eyes in thanksgiving.

'Better.' Miraculously better just for hearing his voice.

'Thank God for that,' said James gruffly. 'Look, this has gone on long enough. You're coming between me and my work. My assistant keeps offering me medication and making noises about a holiday.'

'I'm sorry to hear that,' said Rose, brightening.

'So no more nonsense about giving you more time, lady. Time's up.'

'Yes, James.'

'I should bloody well think so. I'll be with you on Saturday evening, so just make sure your dancecard's empty.'

Rose blinked away the tears that never seemed far away lately. 'Right. I'll do that.'

'But until then I want you to keep one very important fact uppermost in your mind, Rose Sinclair.' James cleared his throat. 'I love you. I always have and I always will.'

Which, thought Rose, as she settled down to sleep, was the only thing that really mattered.

Until that point life had been hard, with everything a chore to be got through as best Rose could manage. But after talking to James her lift in spirits was so visible Bel was euphoric with relief when she arrived next morning. And Minerva, who dropped in later to check on her niece, expressed similar satisfaction when she heard James had been in contact and was coming up at the weekend.

'I take it that after Saturday we can all relax?' she demanded.

Rose nodded. 'I hope so.'

'In which case, Bel dear,' said Minerva, 'you and I must have a little talk. I'll be needing a new manager soon.'

James rang on Saturday from his car to say he'd arrive at seven, by which time Rose had groomed the flat, prepared a simple meal, and had worked herself up into a state of such anticipation she couldn't keep still. When her small French clock struck seven she rushed back to her bedroom to add a few finishing touches to face and hair, then stiffened in horror at the sound of breaking glass somewhere below. Rose raced downstairs to check the shop windows, blew out her cheeks in relief when she found them intact, and went to investigate outside in the arcade.

But as she opened her private door she gasped in astonishment as James thrust a youth through it and slammed the door shut behind him.

'Don't be frightened, darling,' he said swiftly, 'but I think it's time you met your stalker.'

Rose gazed in utter disbelief at the defiant, scarlet-faced boy James was holding by the scruff of his neck. *'Marcus?'*

'So you know him,' said James grimly. 'I thought you might. I caught him red-handed, posting a rose through your door.'

'Get your hands off me,' spat the boy furiously. 'I wasn't doing any harm—'

'Like hell you weren't! You've been frightening my wife to death with your nonsense,' said James with menace. 'You need a good hiding, my lad—'

'Let him go, James,' said Rose, pulling herself together. 'Marcus is Anthony Garrett's son.'

'Lord, I might have known.' James thrust the dishevelled boy away and brushed his hands together, as though ridding himself of contamination, heightening Marcus's colour still further. 'I was just leaving the off-licence when I saw the young idiot sidling towards your door, rose in hand. I collared him, but lost a couple bottles of champagne in the process.'

'So that was the breaking glass I heard.' Rose gazed at the boy, baffled. She knew Marcus Garrett so slightly she had no idea how to deal with the situation. 'Did you send me a card, and make anonymous phone calls too, Marcus?' she asked after a moment, her eyes severe.

'Yes,' he said miserably, white as a sheet now. 'I didn't mean any harm, I swear. I just wanted to—I mean I needed to—' Sudden, racking sobs overtook him, putting an end to his confession.

Rose put an arm round him, pulling a face at James over the boy's dishevelled head. 'James, why not go and buy some more wine while I have a chat with Marcus?'

'Is it safe to do that?' James demanded, eyeing the slim, heaving shoulders with deep distaste. He sighed impatiently as he met the look in her eyes. 'Oh, very well, Rose. If I must. But you behave yourself, laddie,' he warned Marcus. 'I won't be long.'

When James had gone Rose put the distraught youth away from her a little. 'Come into my office, Marcus. I'll give you a drink.'

'Thank you. Sorry to blub like a baby,' he said thickly, following her. 'I suppose you'll tell my father now.'

'It depends.'

By the time Marcus had downed a glass of water, and splashed more on his face, Rose had reached a decision. She fixed the boy with a stern look.

'Right then, Marcus. I've decided I won't tell your father about this.'

His eyes lit with hope, then dulled in despair. 'But he

wants to marry you. You're bound to tell him—' He scowled suddenly. 'Wait a minute. That—that gorilla who mauled me about said you were his *wife*.'

'I am.'

Marcus looked bewildered. 'But you were seeing my father.'

'I've been separated from my husband for a long time,' said Rose gently, 'but we're together again now. Which naturally means I can't go on seeing your father. So I see no need to tell him about this. Or your mother,' she added, startling him. 'But I keep quiet on one condition, Marcus. I need your solemn promise you'll never make phone calls like that again. To anyone. Or keep sending roses all the time.' She shook a finger at him. 'One card, one rose, fine. But to someone more your own age. OK?'

Marcus nodded, then smiled soulfully. 'I'm not sorry about you and Dad. You're loads too young for him. I think you're really cool, Rose.'

'And in any case I'm married to someone else,' said Rose hastily, to stem further outpourings. 'Are you seeing your father tonight?'

Marcus looked at his watch, and swore in a way that would have shocked his parents. 'Sorry! I'm supposed to meet him at the King's Head any minute.'

'Off you go, then.' She opened the office door as she heard James come in. 'We're in here,' she called.

James strode in, carrying a wine-store bag clinking with bottles, his eyes steel-hard as they fastened on the youth. 'Have you called the police yet, Rose?'

'No,' said Rose swiftly, as Marcus turned a sickly shade of green. 'We're settling this out of court, so to speak.' She gave the boy a stern look. 'Right?'

He nodded dumbly, eyes averted from James.

'Right,' said Rose, purposely brisk. 'Have a nice evening with your father, Marcus. And don't worry. I won't say a word, I promise.'

He gazed at her in worshipful gratitude. 'Thanks, Rose, I mean Miss—'

'Mrs Sinclair,' said James very deliberately. 'I'll see you off the premises. And let me add a piece of advice, young Garrett. Make sure you never bother my wife again.'

Rose stayed at the foot of the stairs while James thrust the boy out, then bolted the door. He turned to look at her, with a smile that turned her heart over.

'Are you all right?' he said, as he took her in his arms. 'If that young villain upset you I'll—'

'He didn't, and I'm fine.' she said and kissed him. 'In fact,' she added breathlessly, 'I'm relieved to know it was just Marcus, not someone with something more sinister in mind for me.'

'That's what I thought.' James kissed her at length, then held her close, his cheek rubbing hers for a moment, then to her surprise he picked her up and carried her upstairs.

'I'm not ill any more,' Rose protested, laughing.

'I just like having you in my arms,' he said, grinning, and sat down with her on his lap. 'God, I've missed you!'

Rose returned his kisses with ardour for a moment, then came to a decision. No way was she going to be able to cook dinner, or even just enjoy being with James again, until everything was out in the open for good or ill.

'James,' she said, sitting up to look him in the eye. 'Before we go any further there's something you should know.'

'Is there?' His eyes lit with a surprising gleam. 'Tell me, then.'

Rose swallowed hard, feeling the colour rise in her cheeks. 'Sorry to confront you with the same old problem again, James.' She gazed at him in desperate appeal. 'Though it's not exactly the same problem, because this time—this time I really am pregnant.'

'I know you are, darling,' he said, taking the wind out of her sails. He caught her close, rubbing his cheek against her. 'I've just been waiting for you to tell me.'

'How do you know?' she demanded indignantly, pulling away a little.

'Minerva told me.'

Rose stared at him, utterly dumbstruck.

'When you told me to get lost for a bit I was worried sick,' he said hastily. 'I needed to know how you were, so I rang your aunt. Apparently she thought I had a right to the truth. I *like* your aunt, even though I haven't met her yet,' added James with feeling.

Rose didn't know whether to laugh or cry, so she laughed, and James laughed with her in relief, holding her close.

'I've been in a right old state,' she said unsteadily at last. 'All day I've been rehearsing ways to tell you. And you knew all the time!'

He raised her face to his, his eyes very sober. 'Rose, when I set out to make you fall in love with me again I was ready to go to every length I could to make it happen, but I swear this wasn't part of my plan. But when Minerva gave me the glad news I realised I'd been hoping against hope you might be pregnant. Lord knows, I was too desperate to make love to you again that night to do anything to prevent it.'

'And I never got the chance to tell you I wasn't doing anything to prevent it, either,' she said ruefully, then smiled at him. 'But while we're on the subject I may as well clear up a point or two about this plan of yours, Sinclair. You had no hope of making me fall in love with again, darling, because I'd never fallen *out* of love in the first place.'

With a smothered sound James crushed her close, expressing his appreciation without words, but after a while he put her away from him to look down into her face. 'So clear up another point for me, Rose. Are you truly happy about the baby?'

'Of course I am,' she said joyfully. 'I wanted your baby all those years ago, James. I still do.' To her surprise she saw a trace of moisture in his eyes, and smiled shakily. 'How do you feel about it, Daddy?'

James took so long to tell her exactly how he felt in every detail, it was very late by the time they got round to eating the simple meal Rose had prepared earlier.

'So how soon can you wind things up here and come live with me, sweetheart?' he asked as they lay in each other's arms in bed later.

'Minerva's asked Bel to take over from me, so I'll need to stay to give her a teach-in for a while. After that I'm all yours.'

James gave a great sigh of satisfaction. 'You were mine from the first moment I set eyes on you, sweetheart.'

'Quite a bit before that, actually,' she informed him. 'I took one look at you during a rugby match one Saturday afternoon—'

'At a match?' He frowned. 'I thought you drew my name out of a hat.'

Rose smiled gleefully. 'I did. But I wouldn't have taken part in all that nonsense if I hadn't been madly in love with you to start with, James Sinclair. The three of us were supposed to write different names on each paper, but I wrote yours on all four of mine.'

James gave a shout of laughter and hugged her close. 'Little devil!'

'I still remember the state I was in as Fabia and Con drew other men's names out of the hat.' She smiled radiantly. 'But fate let me draw the slip Fabia had written your name on as a joke, so the others had no idea I'd shortened the odds. You never stood a chance, Sinclair.'

'Am I complaining?' he whispered, and switched off the light.

We're delighted to announce that

A Mediterranean Marriage

is taking place in

HARLEQUIN®
Presents

This month, in THE BELLINI BRIDE by Michelle Reid, #2224

Marco Bellini has to choose a suitable wife.
Will he make an honest woman of his
beautiful mistress, Antonia?

In March you are invited to the wedding of
Rio Lombardi and Holly Samson
in THE ITALIAN'S WIFE by Lynne Graham, #2235

When Holly, a homeless young woman, collapses in front of
Rio Lombardi's limousine, he feels compelled to take her and
her baby son home with him. Holly can't believe it when Rio
lavishes her with food, clothes…and a wedding ring….

Harlequin Presents®
The world's bestselling romance series.
Seduction and passion guaranteed!

Available wherever Harlequin books are sold.

HARLEQUIN®
Makes any time special ®
Visit us at www.eHarlequin.com

Three of romance's most talented craftsmen come together in one special collection.

New York Times bestselling authors

Jayne Ann Krentz

Tess Gerritsen

National bestselling author

Stella Cameron

in

Stolen Memories

With plenty of page-turning passion and dramatic storytelling, this volume promises many memorable hours of reading enjoyment!

Coming to your favorite retail outlet in February 2002.

HARLEQUIN®

Makes any time special ®

Visit us at www.eHarlequin.com

PHSM-MMP

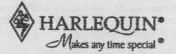

Coming Next Month

HARLEQUIN *Presents*

THE BEST HAS JUST GOTTEN BETTER!

#2229 THE CITY-GIRL BRIDE Penny Jordan
When elegant city girl Maggie Russell is caught in a country flood, rugged Finn Gordon comes to her rescue. He takes her to his farmhouse, laughs at her impractical designer clothes—and then removes them...piece by piece....

#2230 A RICH MAN'S TOUCH Anne Mather
The arrival of businessman Gabriel Webb in Rachel's life is about to change everything! She isn't prepared when he touches emotions in her that she has carefully hidden away. But is Gabriel interested in only a fleeting affair?

#2231 THE PROSPECTIVE WIFE Kim Lawrence
Matt's family are constantly trying to find him a wife, so he is instantly suspicious of blond, beautiful Kat. She's just as horrified to be suspected of being a prospective wife, but soon the talk of bedding and wedding starts to sound dangerously attractive—to both of them....

#2232 HIS MIRACLE BABY Kate Walker
Morgan didn't know why Ellie had left him. It was obvious she'd still been in love with him. But when he found her, to his shock, she had the most adorable baby girl he'd ever seen. Had Ellie found another man or was this baby Morgan's very own miracle?

#2233 SURRENDER TO THE SHEIKH Sharon Kendrick
The last thing Rose expected was to go on assignment to Prince Khalim's kingdom of Maraban. He treated her more like a princess than an employee. Rose knew she could never really be his princess—but their need for each other was so demanding....

#2234 BY MARRIAGE DIVIDED Lindsay Armstrong
Bryn Wallis chose Fleur as his assistant because marriage was definitely not on her agenda—and that suited him perfectly. The last thing he wanted was any romantic involvement. Only, soon he began to find Fleur irresistible....

HPCNM0102